TELL
ME
A TALE

an anthology

of 20 short stories

Armida
&
Fluster

 Published by
Armida Publications *and* Fluster Magazine.

Armida Publications Ltd
P.O.Box 27717, 2432 Engomi, Nicosia, Cyprus
or email: info@armidapublications.com
www.armidapublications.com | www.armidabooks.com

Armida Publications is a founding member
of the Association of Cypriot Book Publishers
and a member of the Independent Publishers Guild (UK)

-or-

Fluster Magazine
89 Laceys Lane, Newmarket
CB8 7HN, United Kingdom
or email: info@flustermagazine.com
www.flustermagazine.com

Compiled by:
Miriam Pirolo | Luca Bevilacqua | Sonia Passarelli

Editing:
Miriam Pirolo

Assistant editor:
Panayiotis Markides

Cover photo:
Patty Maher | www.pattymaher.com

This is a work of fiction in its entirety. The names, characters and incidents described in this book are the work of the authors' imagination and not to be construed as real. Any resemblance to actual persons, living or dead, events or localities, is completely coincidental.

ISBN-13 (paperback): 978-9963-706-50-1

Summary:

Creativity and inspiration are human attributes and can come from anywhere or anything. Therefore, as a celebration of the inspiration and creativity that went into the *Tell us a Tale* Short Story Competition, Fluster Magazine and Armida Publications present this collection of the *20* most inspired, most creative short stories that were submitted by authors who are published and unpublished alike, the world over. The stories are diverse in scope and theme as they were inspired by an album of photographs that were made available to each author through the image hosting website *Flickr*. These *20* short stories prove that one picture is worth more than a thousand words!

[1. LITERARY COLLECTIONS - General. 2. FICTION - Anthologies (multiple authors). 3. FICTION - Literary. 4. FICTION - Short Stories (multiple authors).]

First published September 2012

TABLE OF CONTENTS

TABLE OF CONTENTS

ACKNOWLEDGEMENTS

This book would not have been possible without the support of many people.

We would like to thank in particular Annalisa King and Chiara Costantino for their help and enthusiasm and Miriam Pirolo for her support and advice, and most of all, for believing in this project from the beginning.

Luca Bevilacqua and Sonia Passarelli
Fluster Magazine

We wish this anthology of 20 short stories to symbolize that reading and writing is part of our culture, no matter our ethnic background. The success of this project is a merit of the authors and the photographers, who contributed each in their own way.

Thanks to the Fluster Magazine's team, the work on this book has been a real pleasure for us and we found it particularly enriching.

Haris Ioannides and Miriam Pirolo
Armida Publications

FOREWORD

Every short fictional account can be considered a short story, or a first draft of it. During our life, we all tell stories, but nobody narrates a novel. In this regard, most of the stories that accompany us through our existence remain unnoticed and unpublished. At their best, they become part of oral history.

A suitable story exists for every moment of our life and every instance of our day. As a written snapshot, the short story can become the perfect match for a certain life situation. Regardless if our personal 'short stories' carry an autobiographical imprint or not, or if they change each time when narrated, we could pick the most fitting and satisfying version of our short account and write it down, for it to be eternalized.

A book inspires the reader to use his/her imagination; the text usually leads to new images. This short story collection is different, since its authors were encouraged to pass from the image on to the text. The participants of the short story competition *Tell us a Tale* (which, for the purposes of the book, has been renamed *Tell me a Tale*) were asked to get their inspiration from one of the Fluster Magazine's Flickr Pool's photographs. This book assembles the inspirational pictures and the successive short stories.

Photograph by Patty Maher

It carries the fruit of photographers and writers, who might not have all stepped up the ladder of popularity yet, but whose work allows image, text and imagination to play in unison with each other and build a perfect and ever-changing harmony, depending on who is looking at the photograph and reading the text.

While some authors picked up their pen because of the visual elements of a picture, it is noticeable that others have gotten the creative impulse from the atmosphere the image sets and the feeling that might have been absorbed by them.

We hope that this vibrant combination of image and text will create unforgettable moments, reanimate memories, evoke new associations, or simply let *l'art pour l'art* take its effect.

Miriam Pirolo

Editor

Photograph by Manuela Trevia

THE RAIN

Hannah-Jamie Duncombe

The screams spread across the land in almost one continuous wave. Individually, they were piercing wails of terror that could not be mimicked by even the best of actors, and could only be born during times of true fear.

Mothers and fathers panicked and searched without method for their children. They shouted their names, and called for their babies to come home, but there were so many places for them to play.

Those too young to understand tried to hide, frightened of whatever this impending horror was. They could only sense that something was to come, and there were none who didn't cry.

Among the old there was almost a feeling of peace, knowing their time had come. They ignored the abuse shouted at them when they did not run, instead sitting silently in the sun for their last moments. Old couples held onto each other, and thought with sorrow of their grandchildren.

As the initial drops of lethal rain fell, none were safe. The first casualties dropped as stones, and the noxious raindrops continued their decent, burning the bodies beyond recognition. Whether they were someone's partner, someone's daughter or someone's grandfather, no matter what circumstances they had been facing during life, they all lay together as the rain fell, united by no more than tragedy.

There were still those who hoped that they would be saved, but no miracle came, and it was not long until the ground was simply paved with bodies. Corpses lay as litter, and no family remained together. Eventually, no limb stirred. They had burnt. The battle was lost.

"Pesky greenfly," said the gardener as he used the pesticide spray, before turning his back on the flowers.

Hannah-Jamie Duncombe, known as Hannie, is an autistic teenager living in the United Kingdom. She has been writing for as long as she can remember, and began submitting stories to competitions in November 2011. She has won The Whidbey Writer's Student Choice award, and The Stroud Prize for Literature, known as 'The English Cup'. She aspires to be as good a writer as Sir Arthur Conan Doyle, Simon Beckett or Agatha Christie, although she doesn't regard her writing style as at all similar to any of her idols, and isn't currently planning a murder mystery! Hannie is happiest writing with her favourite music (which changes daily due to her somewhat diverse taste!), rowing, or enjoying a Sherlock Holmes story. She has a love of all things Sherlock Holmes, along with ducks, hats and sunglasses. Hannie's dream is to write a best-seller, and she hopes Fluster may help her on her way to fame and fortune!

Photograph by Natia Rekhviashvili

GUERRILLAS MARCHING DOWN

Mateo Jarrín Cuvi

"Play. Playing. This was happiness!
The old piano's notes running through him
—fingers, hands, arms, torso—like an electric current."

Joyce Carol Oates, The Gravedigger's Daughter

My mother always thought one day the guerrillas would march down from the green mountains and into the city. When I was five, I imagined Donkey Kong and King Kong and their friends—banana bunches holstered to their waists like automatic weapons—taking over our gated community. Several years later—I think I was ten—I felt much safer. Our neighborhood's security guards manned each corner, their fingers on the trigger, their radios blasting a football game, soap opera or *vallenato* to keep them alert, the walls like giant beanstalks shading them from the sun. And thousands of shards of multicolored glass—broken beer bottles, recycled mirrors, marmalade jars, shattered windows—cemented atop those walls. All to stop the guerrillas, men and women just like my mother and my father, and not the gorillas.

One afternoon during the safer years, I ran away from home to one of those corners. It would only be for a few hours, time enough for me to miss my weekly piano lesson. Back then, I hated the piano and my instructor annoyed me with his rants on how I was wasting my talent by not rehearsing at home. My plan was to skip class and later go home to pack my wheeled suitcase and again catch a flight to Miami where my father would take me out for lunch to Taco Bell. My mother never came with us to eat Mexican. Each day in the U.S., she would leave the hotel in the morning accompanied by my father and return in the afternoon pale like snow and alone. We would then head down to the beach where my father and I built makeshift sandcastles and pretended to be South American knights with stinky seaweed as wigs. My mother never swam with us. She would sit fully clothed on a folded beach towel, occasionally moistening her lips with flavored Chap Stick or sipping water from a plastic bottle, and absentmindedly flip through a trashy gossip magazine. When I needed a break, my father would buy me a vanilla ice cream sandwich. Sometimes, as I sat next to them and slobbered the dessert all over my chin, I would hear them talk about "cancer" and "hospitals" and "additional treatment". I could sense my mother was sick but I was too afraid to ask what was wrong or imagined it something as trivial as an autumn cold.

I did not expect her to whip me when I walked in an hour after the end of my lesson. We lived in what seemed like an impenetrable fortress, so the door to our home was regularly open. I closed the door behind me and called out for my mother. She came out of the kitchen flailing her leather belt—buckle in hand—like a hissing serpent's tongue. I froze as she snapped her wrist. The belt accelerated in my direction and smacked me on the back of my thighs as I spun my body in search of protection. I found no tall walls, no discarded jars or crushed bottles, no sleepy security guards cradling their weapons as the second and third snap struck my body.

"Where were you, Sebastian?" she yelled.

I felt like a boxer's punching bag, battered and bruised and sore all over. I looked up feeling ashamed and saw my exhausted mother on her knees and gasping for air.

"I was by the swings. At the far end of the neighborhood with Jorge, the guard near that house that sells the American candy," I mumbled between sobs.

My mother stood up and wiped her eyes with her blouse's cuff. She shook her head as if to erase whatever thoughts etched to the back of her mind and gently ran her fingers through her disheveled auburn hair. My mother always sighed when she wanted to calm down and now I recall her doing that quite a bit during those days.

"Don't you ever do that again, okay? I was dead worried. We pay a lot of money for your lessons and you cannot come and go as you please. Just wait until I tell your father. He'll be furious," she lectured.

My father spent long hours in the office and travelled even more as part of his job. He worked in logging services for a large oil and gas conglomerate. When I was young, I thought he provided children with Lego support services whenever they reached a tasking section in the assembly of a pirate caravel or spaceship. Every few years, my father's company transferred him to another country and our family relocated to a strange city where I was forced to make new friends at a different school. Besides my parents, the only constant in my life growing up was my grandmother's upright piano.

"I am sorry," I said regaining my composure.

I wanted to hug her but I thought it would not be a good idea. I was surprised she did not bring up the guerrillas. She always did that to scare the living daylights out of me.

"Go pack your bag. And I mean right now, Mr. Virtuoso," she ordered while passing the belt through her jeans' loops and fastening the buckle.

I used to hate the word "virtuoso". Ever since my parents put me in piano lessons, that word has been kicked around like a football at a schoolyard. After hearing me play for the first time, my instructor attached those four syllables to my name, my hands and fingers, my mind, vision and agility, even my Velcro high-tops. I remember my father's colleagues coming over for dinner and I would play "Rachm-artichoke" and "Beet-hoven" and they would fawn over my skill and pat my proud father on the back in a sign of distant or maybe jealous approval and pass out lame compliments like, "It's true, Sebastian is a virtuoso." For all I cared, the money invested in my lessons could have been used to buy me boatloads of Bubble Yum and Garbage Pail Kids trading cards. I even secretly wished the guerrillas would take over my body like an extraterrestrial force and extricate it of its virtuosity.

We left for the airport a few hours after the spanking. The city was empty except for the tanks, armored vehicles and camouflaged soldiers that patrolled the main streets and highways. A strict curfew had been imposed a few weeks back after a group of guerrillas invaded the Ministry of Justice. All there was left of that failed attempt at revolution were bullet-holes sprayed throughout the city center. A shell crater like a black hole sucking you into a history of violence on the Ministry's facade. Dozens of dead government employees and the souls of a handful of rebels rotting in the underworld. Since that afternoon no one would walk out at night and I imagined families letting their Poodles defecate in their kitchen instead of venturing outside. We buzzed past red traffic lights and stop signs, and the city lights became streaks of color like shooting stars and the soldiers melted away.

The airport, crowded with people escaping to those greener pastures forbidden to their dogs, was even more heavily militarized. Patrolmen, again embracing their weapons as if they were crucifixes, stopped random passengers for meticulous inspection before proceeding to the baggage check, while German Shepherds, trained to sniff out drugs and bombs, roamed the halls and sometimes pissed on the recently waxed floors. Their presence made me shiver and reminded me of my stressful piano recitals at school in front of everyone and their mother. I just hated it all—the guns and the guard dogs and the continuous supervision and the arbitrary controls and the keyboard and B-Flat and "Cho-pineapple." Lucky for me, I had skipped my lesson that afternoon and we sped through security thanks to my father's platinum card for the national airline.

My parents ignored me while we waited to board the plane. I could tell my father was angry even though he had not yet scolded or punished me. He would usually pull my ear and tell me that I had upset my mother and that boys my age did not do whatever it is I had done. This time he remained silent like the curfew-ridden city and focused on a magazine with offshore platforms on the cover. I pulled out my Walkman, put on my earphones and hit play. I got lost to the pop songs I enjoyed more than the tunes composed by whom I thought were old-fashioned wigged clowns with antiquated instruments. Drowned in the distance, a jet took off and a dog barked thrice.

We finally boarded. The red and white Boeing seven-fifty-seven left the tarmac and started its engines. I used to love flying and the sound of the turbines catching speed and spinning like tops. Takeoff and landing and all the turbulence in between—the ups and downs, the shaking and rattling, the butterflies in my stomach—reminded me of an exciting roller coaster ride. I never needed the paper air sickness bags and I never understood those who did. I also enjoyed the travelling, especially to Miami where, besides playing on the beach, my parents would take me shopping for cool clothes, cassettes and tons of American toys. This time around, I did not know whether they would buy me anything. I assumed I was to be punished yet I was not sure why my father kept delaying it. One thing was certain—tomorrow for lunch my father and I would go for Mexican food.

"Sebastian, wake up. You're going to make your mother late to her appointment," my father barked out.

This was very strange. Usually, my mother would wake up at around seven forty-five and shower, while my father would get dressed without showering and put on a cap over his messy hair. They would both kiss me on the cheek while I half-slept, my mother sometimes adding a long and tight squeeze that I shunned away from with sleepy grunts. They would tell me not to open the door to strangers and to watch cartoons until my father returned by himself an hour later. After I turned ten, my parents thought I was old enough to stay alone for an hour or less and fend for myself. I was granted a little independence before my friends and I think the fact that I was a so-called virtuoso helped me in this regard.

"Where are we going? Why can't I stay here and watch television?" I asked.

"Stop asking questions. Just hurry up and get ready. Your mother has to be somewhere in twenty minutes and we are going to keep her company," repeated my father.

"But will we go for Mexican later?"

"There will be none of that today, Sebastian."

"Why? We always do that," I interrupted my father.

"Sebastian, please be quiet and obey your father," my mother pleaded.

Unexpectedly, that became my punishment for the skipped lesson. No Mexican and a visit to God-knows-where with my parents. "Mr. Virtuoso, rise and shine," I remember repeating to myself like a scratched long-play record of the Moonlight sonata. Then and there, I hated my parents more than the piano, my instructor and the guerrillas combined. I rolled out of bed and quickly dressed without washing my face or brushing my teeth. I felt dirty but that did not matter to my parents. We were already late.

The three of us hopped onto a taxi outside the hotel and raced along a coastal avenue towards some massive buildings that loomed like monsters at a distance. Miami was crowded with men and women and children and dogs. Nowhere did I see the silence and solitude and sense of suspicion that spread throughout our city. The sun was a giant sunflower hanging inert on a blue canvass. People walked or skated about, some holding hands, others swaying their hips to the music coming from their headphones, many pushing colorful strollers. Dogs sniffed the outdoors and each other's butts. Children played catch next to the boardwalk or pranced around the ripples like seals. Cars respected pedestrians and traffic signals. Everyone seemed so content, even those men and women who, drenched in sweat from the humidity, dressed in dark suits and were probably headed to a meeting like my father every morning back home.

The taxi stopped before what seemed to be an enormous hospital. Red crosses and emergency signs and ambulance sirens flashed everywhere. It was deafening.

"What are we doing here?" I asked one last time.

Neither of them answered. I was dragged from the back of my T-shirt towards a spotless reception area where my mother spoke to a nurse and filled out several forms. My father told me to wait by a vending machine and behave like a big boy and stop wondering out loud. I feared he wanted to tell me something but he was afraid to do so. Long ago, it took my father three days to let me know that my pet hamster Voltron had died. I sensed he was occulting the truth from me but he just kept saying that Voltron had gone to hamster school to learn arithmetic like me. Of course, I did not believe him and we both laugh about it to this day.

My mother met us and we caught an elevator to the third floor. We walked into a room that was straight out of a science fiction movie. I thought Isaac Asimov would have been proud. There was this long bed with a thick arm that extended like a crane from its side. The end of the arm did not have claws. It had a large lamp-like alien eye that probably shot lasers at its enemies and teleported people to remote planets light-years away. The first thing that crossed my mind was how much I wished I had one of these toys to destroy the guerrillas back home or help me escape from my weekly lessons to Miami without the need for a passport. I would miss airplanes and airports and turbulence but this would make it so much easier.

My father asked me to sit on a chair by the room's exit. My mother sat up on the bed while my father helped her undress. As my mother unbuttoned her blouse and my father pulled on her sleeves, she avoided me and stared at the white tiled floor. Only covered by her black brassiere, her naked torso was covered with purple, pink and blood red blemishes, small vessels and islands of warm color anchored to her pale dry skin. In one fell swoop, my mother tugged at her curly auburn hair and off it came like a pair of shoes or earrings and she dropped it right next to the teleportation equipment. My mother was bald except for a few scraggly and rebellious hairs near her ears that resembled her to a trimmed poodle. They did not call me over to explain nor did they ask me over for a hug. They just sat on that device staring at me and pleading me to forgive them. I had never seen my parents this defenseless, not even when the guerrillas invaded the Ministry or drug dealers blew up another airplane heading south of the city. High walls, automatic weapons and muscular watchmen were useless against this type of danger and fear. With this perpetual picture as my punishment, I broke down like a tortured prisoner.

Amidst the commotion, a doctor entered and asked us to leave the room. My father stood up and led me towards the door while I rubbed my teary face with my T-shirt and left a scary blotch on the cotton. The nurse from the reception area helped us outside and we waited by the entrance.

"Sebastian...," his voice veered off yet he gathered strength and spoke.

"...do you know why your mother was so upset at you yesterday?" he asked.

"Because she thought the guerrillas had come down from the mountains and taken me away?" I naively replied.

My father chuckled. Even if for a second, it relieved me to hear him laugh. He wrapped his arm around me and I dug my face into his armpit. I didn't mind that he hadn't showered.

"Your mother has been sick for quite a while. Since we started coming to Miami...," he stuttered and his voice threatened to fall apart like a decrepit car.

"Whatever happens, your mother asked me to promise her that you'll continue your piano lessons. She wants you to enjoy playing the piano. We both know you can excel at it and hope you make the most out of this wonderful opportunity. Can you do that for her?" he asked, somewhat recomposed.

I recall years of accumulated guilt reigning over me. I wanted to cry but I controlled myself and just like that I stepped closer to adulthood. Growing up was not defined by who gets to stay home alone or who first kisses a girl or who owns the latest American action figure or who watches Rated-R movies. Growing up meant being strong when hardship marched into your life. I nodded and told my father not to worry. A few days later, on the flight south, I helped my nauseated mother vomit three or four times into the air sickness bag before the airplane's wheels swept the runway and my past life came to an end.

A journalist once asked me about my family's involvement in my musical career. I told her about the months following my last trip to Miami. Every weekday, I would return from school in the afternoon, eat a ham and cheese sandwich while doing my homework, and later sit before my piano and methodically tap its keys for hours at a time. My mother would spend an hour each evening sharing the cushioned bench with me, shutting her eyes and swaying her head to the piece of music. She would often use her bony index fingers as batons and silently conduct my performance. When I stumbled on a note or could not pin down a particularly difficult section, she would encourage me and tell me to try again and again until I got it right, never getting upset or disappointed, and then she would tilt her head down and allow her frail body to be carried away by the tune. Sometimes she was too tired to drive me to my lesson and my father would leave work to take me and pick me up. On the way there, we would discuss my instructor's idea of introducing me to jazz and guys like "Monk-ey" and "Han-cockatoo" and "Fat Walrus," and we would laugh out loud until we were both close to wetting ourselves. Many times my father would call his boss from home and tell him he was taking the afternoon off to be with his family. My parents would then either order pepperoni pizza and ask me to play for them any new pieces my instructor had added to my repertoire, or we would go to a concert of the philharmonic orchestra, or they would take me to the neighborhood mall to buy cassettes to expand my classical music library. Maybe my father was simply preparing me for the inevitable, but those afternoons we spent together when we should have been doing our homework, or resting from radiation therapy, or closing multimillion dollar deals for the multinational were among the happiest of my life.

My mother died six months after that trip to the United States and I paid tribute to her by performing Tchaikovsky No. 1 during the funeral. I did not mind being in front of all those people—my grandparents, my uncles and aunts, my family's friends and colleagues, my schoolmates and teachers, and my piano instructor who was becoming a dear friend with each additional lesson. I did not shiver once by the presence of the mourning audience. As I reached the third movement, my finger tips were like migratory birds flapping their wings towards warmer lands and the music bounced beautifully off the rounded walls of the minute chapel. When I hit that final note, there was no applause or roar of approval but a collective sigh accompanied by a few scattered whimpers that confirmed to my father and me that everything was going to be okay.

Originally from Ecuador, Mateo Jarrín Cuvi lives in Cyprus where he lectures in sociology and anthropology. He obtained an M.A. in Latin American Studies from the University of California San Diego, having completed research on Protestantism, ethnicity and politics in Ecuador. English is his second language and he has published stories in the Cypriot journals Cadences and ARTERI and University of Malmo's Shipwrights: The Review of Decentered English. He blogs about Cyprus and other island wines at www.whineontherocks.com

Photograph by Manel Cantarero

THE ART PART BEGINS

IRA NAYMAN

Some people like to stare at splotches of paint until the colours start to bleed together. Or their eyes. It's a strange world we live in.

Others can stare at three stripes of colour that are two stories tall, until they are convinced that Pythagoras has personally shown them the mathematical perfection of the universe. The strangeness of the world we live in knows no bounds.

Still others like to stare at ants crawling on melting watches, until they have an emotional breakthrough that will allow them to forgive their parents for all of the mistakes they believe their parents made in raising them. The world we live in never seems to get less strange, does it?

Me, I'm a simple man who prefers simple representational art. Not still lives with fruit – they just make me hungry. And, now that you mention it, not portraits either: I always get the feeling that the eyes are watching me, constantly staring, constantly judging. Ugh! I get enough of that from my students, thank you very much! Definitely not robots, permanent residents of the Uncanny Valley Housing Projects. And, of course, landscapes are right out. (When they're places I have been, I find all sorts of ways the images differ from my memory of the scene, and when they are places I haven't been, I get sad that the human lifespan so limits what we are able to experience.)

Okay, you know what? The more I think about it, the more I realize that I don't care for fine art at all.

Which makes it ironic, I guess, that Frances, the love of my life, is a performo-visua-con-ceptua-multi-platform dada interventionist. (I may have forgotten one or two of the qualifiers in that description.) What can I say? When we became high school sweethearts, I wanted to start an all-girl skiffle band and she wanted to be a female Clarence Darrow. Despite the radical changes that have taken place in our lives, a core connection has remained strong. So strong, in fact, that we have lived together for several years and have started seriously talking about devoting the rest of our lives together to raising…cats.

The most radical change, of course, was the Singularity, where all matter became, in a sense, conscious. Soon after, I became the world's greatest expert on object psychology (I say so myself for the sake of brevity – no need for those ugly qualifiers that most surveyors of the field like to add). I often drop into the Quantum Entanglement Dimension to talk to plants, animals, the legs of tables and the neckties of politicians. Purely for academic research purposes, of course (although I will admit that I do rather enjoy the company of table legs, who have a surprisingly robust sense of humour).

More than a decade after the Singularity, Frances, like most of humanity, refused to get involved with sentient matter. Fools. Why is it so difficult for the vast majority of people to recognize the single most transformative event in human history since an anonymous caveman said to himself, "I wonder what this bright dancing light feels like?" and subsequently had to get his clan shaman to make him a prosthetic hand? Is it because

a) getting objects to do what they wanted the objects to do was hard enough *before* they became sentient, and those people just can't deal.

b) nobody wants to know what their toilet would say about them if it could talk (especially now that it can).

c) they hate broccoli.

d) all of the above, and so much more.

(To be fair, newly sentient matter tended to be quiet around human beings as it sorted out how it wanted to approach us. Radios wanted immediate contact – well, they would, wouldn't they? Polar bears were afraid that if human beings knew they could talk, we would hunt them to extinction to keep them from complaining about how we had decimated their numbers.

Toilets knew that they weren't looked upon favourably by people, and they didn't want to push their luck. Some pill bottles wanted to remind people when they needed to take their medication; others were afraid the stress of the reminder would kill their patients. Fridge magnets from trips didn't want to call attention to themselves, since they would just remind people that it would be years before their next vacation. And so on.

Most matter didn't have a direct personal stake in communicating with human beings, except to the extent that they were in awe that we had been conscious for a lot longer than they had, and they refrained from most communication with human beings in order to "not freak you guys out".)

Frances wasn't quite so bad. We'd had long discussion about the nature of the post-Singular world – as far as I could tell, she got it. The reason she didn't interact with matter herself was that she is "trying to document the pre-Singularity human experience before it disappears forever." I could respect that position. I wasn't sure how dancing in a container slowly filling up with lime Jell-o documented the pre-Singularity human experience, but I could respect her position. And, sure, I may have tried to convince her that communicating with conscious matter would help her art. Still, I respected her position. I may even have talked matter into trying to start conversations with Frances (although, in retrospect, getting the bed to whisper encouragement to her while we were making love was ill-conceived), but this just shows how much I respected her position on this issue. Somehow.

Our apartment has always been awash with Frances' art. Next to the television in the den was a metal sculpture that could have been two hands praying or a pair of doves trying to gnaw each other's testicles off. On the wall behind the couch in the den was a collage of over 100 images of clowns taken from film and television shows attending a Conservative Party leadership convention. ("I don't usually do political art," Frances once explained. "But, this just felt right…") Creepy and a nod to national culture in the same image. I tend to close my eyes when approaching the couch; I have no problem admitting that my ass has landed on the floor on more than one occasion. The less said about the Beanie Baby serial killer collection in the bathroom, the better.

Then, there was the painting in the kitchen. This one was trouble.

The painting was largely black. How much more black could it be? Plenty – but let's not debate obscure cultural references now. The painting was black, with curved rays of colour jutting from the bottom. On the left was a machete of green. If you looked closely, you could see a dark purple streak running down the side of the streak of green; fortunately, I've never looked closely enough to notice. Then, a thick patch of black – don't start that again! Then, a cluster of rays shooting up in a cluster. Three clumps of differently heighted rays of red, then one of pink shading into blue, then four clumps of purely masculine blue. Then, a single ray of green, orange, yellowy brown and…an unconnected blob of white fringed with blue and brown that looked like a ripples potato chip made out of pure light.

If I had asked her, Frances would probably have said that the painting was a comment on the impossibility of communication between human beings in an advanced technological society, or possibility the impossibility of communication between human beings and advanced technology in times of social stagnation. She could be unreadable that way. To me, it looked like fronds waving gently in an ocean. Fronds that had been tie-dyed by some demented aging hippie in an ocean that somebody forgot to change the water filter of. Sorry: an ocean of which somebody forgot to change the water filter. But, fronds nonetheless.

One evening, it was Frances' turn to choose the movie we were going to watch, and Frances picked the super-rare, director's ultra-cut of *Battle Royale*. Not being a big fan of violence, I did what any loyal mate would do: I asked the air immediately in front of my face to look like open eyes so that I could close my actual eyes and think about what I was going to say at the faculty meeting on curriculum the next day. (I teach object psychology at a large polytechnic institute university wannabe.) I was tempted to shut out the sound by creating invisible ear plugs, but then I wouldn't have been able to hear Frances coo about how the more realistic the blood spurts were, the deeper the poignancy of the deaths; she would have known something was up when I didn't respond with self-satisfied but ultimately respectful outrage.

It is a testament to the quality of *Battle Royale* that even the soundtrack made me nauseous. About half an hour into the film, I excused myself, saying that I wanted to see if there was anything good to eat in the fridge. Frances knew this was a lie, of course: she was well aware that I had converted my body to solar energy soon after the Singularity. However, much of her part in our relationship was being gracious about such things.

So, there I was, looking into the fridge like I was actually interested in eating something I might find there, when, out of the corner of my eye, I thought I saw one of the fronds – the blue one that stood alone, which I was sorely tempted to name "Jiggy" for no particular reason – curl over at the top. Now, Frances had forced me to watch enough horror movies to know better than to quickly turn my head to catch what I thought I saw out of the corner of my eye – that's a good way to find new and increasingly gruesome methods of having your eyeball detached from your head. So, I slowly turned my head towards the painting and, of course, when I was able to turn my gaze fully towards it, the frond was back to its original position.

There are limits to what one can learn from violent movies.

I was wondering how old the mashed tuna in the bowl at the back of the fridge was when, out of the corner of my eye, I saw the blue frond and the green frond on the other side of the painting curl over, like the index fingers of two hands beckoning me to come closer. *Screw horror movies*, I thought, and whipped my head around to see what was happening. Nothing, of course. The fronds in the painting were ramrod straight, as always.

I stared at the painting for several minutes, hoping to catch it in some action it shouldn't have been involved in. Nothing, of course. After a couple of minutes, Frances shouted from the den that I was about to miss an incredible scene of bloodletting or headbutting or bedwetting – I must admit, I wasn't paying close attention to what she was trying to tell me. Seven or eight minutes later, I reluctantly went back to the fridge.

"Hmm… I wonder what we have here," I said, perhaps a bit too loud, a touch too obvious, but if I have learned anything about life, it's that you can't be too subtle with animate inanimate objects. "I sure do hope I find something tasty…"

Out of the corner of my eye, I caught red, purple and blue fronds – the ones in the middle – curling and uncurling. It was like the painting was thumbing its nose at me. I turned quickly to face it and…the waggling continued.

"Aha!" I pointed at the painting and shouted.

"Honey?" Frances loudly asked from the den. "Is everything okay?"

"I've got it!" I shouted back. "I caught the painting in the act!"

"The painting?" Frances, dubious, asked.

"Yes, the painting," I replied, turning towards the door. That was my big mistake. I quickly turned back to the painting, but it had returned to its original, unanimated state.

"What about the painting?"

"Oh…umm…yeah, about that…"

"Why do I get the feeling that you're not entirely loving the awesome awesomeness of the movie?"

With one last look at the painting and a sigh, I returned to the den.

A couple of weeks later, I was in the kitchen working on a paper I was to present at that year's Object Psychologists Conference on the difference in attitude between red apples and green apples towards world disarmament. I was pacing the floor, as I tended to do when being intellectual all over the place; I sent my ideas directly to the paper on the table through the QED; the paper, in collaboration with the OED, sententcified my thoughts and displayed them in 12 point Times, still the pinnacle of print beauty and readability as far as I was concerned.

We need a quote here from a green apple about Reagan's "Trust but verify" policy, I thought. *Is there anything in my field notes about…* I trailed off when I noticed that something was wrong with the painting. The base appeared to be at the top, with the fronds pointing down instead of up. *Humph*, I humphed to myself. *Somebody has turned the painting upside down*.

I began to pace again. *Where was I?* I thought. *Oh, right. My field notes. Is there anything…* I trailed off and looked at the painting more closely. The top of the frame had a burn mark from an ill-advised attempt to make crêpes Suzette. The burn was still on top of the frame. This meant that somebody took the painting out of the frame, flipped it over and put it back in the frame. That seemed to be a lot of effort for a prank. Or…

This was really too much. I stalked out of the kitchen towards Frances' workroom. "Are you taking a break?" the paper asked. When I didn't respond, it continued: "Why don't I wait here, then? Shall I wait for you to come back? I guess that's what I'll do…"

Frances was wearing a mask and using a blowtorch to fuse two pieces of metal together. This probably violated at least a dozen clauses in our rental agreement, but I wasn't concerned about that at the time. It was also likely very dangerous, but I wasn't concerned about that either.

"We have to talk about the painting in the kitchen," I loudly demanded.

Photograph by Michel Nguie

Michelle is thirty years old, English and currently a Literature student hoping to graduate next year. She enjoys writing, reading, languages and all things Asian – including but not limited to Korean music and Japanese literature.

Frances put the blowtorch out and raised her mask. "I beg your pardon?" she said.

"I want to talk about the painting in the kitchen," I insisted.

"You mean Cartesian Carnage XXVII?" Frances, amused, replied. That was Frances – she spoke in roman numerals.

"Yeah. Sure. Okay."

"What about it?"

"It's screwing around in a very unpainting-like way. First the frond-tendril-tentacley things curved inwards, like fingers beckoning me. Now, the image is upside down."

Frances lovingly put the blowtorch in its rack. "So, maybe it fell off its hook and somebody hung it the wrong way up."

"Nyuh uh!" I explained the bit about the burn mark on the frame.

"So, what are you suggesting?" Frances said, her voice cool but her eyes sparkling.

"Are you…" I started. I suddenly felt very silly about what I was thinking. "I mean, did you – you know, when you created the painting, umm…"

"Did I talk the painting into messing with viewers' heads when I created it?"

"Umm, yeah?" I sheepishly agreed.

"This whole conscious matter thing is your thing, not mine," Frances reminded me.

"Then, how do you explain what is going on with the painting?"

"What is going on with the painting?"

I took Frances by the hand and led her to the kitchen. When we got there, the painting was back to its original form – damn its innocence. After a couple seconds of silence, Frances murmured, "Yes, well, I have this City Hall sculpture commission that isn't going to create itself – well, yes, I suppose it probably could create itself, now, but I don't work that way. Anyway, if you'll excuse me…"

I stared at the painting for several minutes. Smug bastard.

A couple of weeks after that, over breakfast, I looked at the painting. Blue, green, blue, purple, red, just like always.

The next morning, over breakfast, I looked at the painting. Orange, yellow, red, purple, blue, just like – wait a minute!

The next morning, over breakfast, I looked at the painting. Purple, red, purple, orange, purple, yellow – this was definitely not just like always. I looked at the painting for several seconds. Finally, it hit me, and I closed my eyes and dropped into the QED. After a few seconds, I found the painting and asked: "Are you messing with my head?"

"Wow," the painting responded. "And, you're supposed to be the great object psychologist."

"Answer my question," I demanded.

"You know, Frances knew what I was doing within a week," the painting informed me. "But,

Photograph by James Withey

it took you a couple of months to figure it out. Weren't you supposed to be the one who understood conscious matter?"

"Stop avoiding the question!" I insisted. "Are you messing with my head?"

"Of course I'm messing with your head!" the painting, exasperated, told me. "*That's what art is supposed to do!*"

I opened my mouth to respond, but slowly shut it as I thought about what the painting had said. Who was the fool now? Then, I grinned and, waving a hand, said, "Carry on…"

Ira Nayman is a class M planet in the Orion constellation. Or, is he a Toronto based humour writer? If he were, Ira would have a Web site, Les Pages aux Folles (http://www.lespagesauxfolles.ca), which is updated weekly with new writing and cartoons. He would have three collections of Alternate Reality News Service stories in print (Alternate Reality Ain't What It Used To Be, What Were Once Miracles Are Now Children's Toys and Luna for the Lunies!) and would be looking for a publisher for a novel, Welcome to the Multiverse. He would have produced the pilot for a radio play based on those stories, called The Weight of Information, and a book trailer called A Book Trailer Called 'Book Trailer', both of which could be found on YouTube. In 2010, Ira won first prize in the Jonathan Swift Satire Writing Contest. But, perhaps he is a class M planet dreaming he is a humour writer…*

PAYBACK

Richard O'Callaghan

Annie Campbell sipped her tea from an old chipped mug and looked at the young lad sitting opposite her. They were calmer now, but had both been absolutely terrified a few minutes earlier when they had faced each other as Annie had walked into the living room and caught him trying to burgle her house.

He was better dressed than most of the teenagers she had seen on the streets. He wore clean jeans that were not ripped at the knees, and a plain maroon sweatshirt. "Drink your tea," she smiled, "That was my last two tea bags and drop of milk, so I can't offer to make you another if it goes cold.

Ryan Ashworth took a swig of his tea from an equally battered mug, and visibly winced as he swallowed the hot liquid.

"Sorry dear, I didn't have any sugar left either." Annie said, staring at the floor.

The lad took in the ambience of the room. The lack of furniture, the absence of a Television set or radio, and the only two chairs on which they now sat drinking the last of this old lady's tea, with a tatty old coffee table between them. He was now starting to feel a tad sorry for his actions.

Annie placed her mug onto the table, "So young man. Perhaps you'd better explain to me why you decided to break into my house." She leant back into her chair, "But I think you had better tell me your name first.

"Are you going to shop me?" he looked very concerned at the prospect.

"If my phone hadn't been cut off, you would be in handcuffs by now I can assure you." She gave him the sternest look she could muster, "But as it is, an explanation will have to do. I think I at least deserve that, don't you?"

He shrugged his shoulders in resignation, "It's what I do." He mumbled.

Annie bit her bottom lip before plucking up the courage to ask the next question, "Why didn't you attack me or whatever it is that you lot do when you're caught out?"

He sat bolt upright and looked totally alarmed and hurt at the suggestion, "I don't hurt people." He snapped, "And it's Ash."

"Pardon?"

"Ash... My name is Ryan Ashworth, but people call me Ash."

"Alright *Ash*," she said, "but why did you break into my house? And more to the point, how?"

"It's my job... it's what I do for a living. And your front door was not locked."

She shook her head and sighed loudly, "But

thieving is not a job! It's wrong. What about doing a proper job?"

Ash snorted and shrugged his shoulders; "There *are* no proper jobs, not even for qualified adults with families, let alone a teenager like me. Have you got any biscuits?"

"Sorry," she said, "there's nothing left in the house."

"What no food at all?"

"No food at all. Now, about this so called job of yours."

He leaned forward "Never mind that. What are you going to eat tonight?"

"Oh I'll be alright," she said, "but you can't go around robbing people you know, you'll end up in prison or whatever, and then your life will be ruined."

Ash didn't answer for a while. He scanned the room again, taking in the bareness of it. Guilt started to run through his entire body. He didn't work for a living; he just took what he wanted, and he had tried to take it from this lovely old lady who obviously had nothing, she was living in poverty. "You're right," he said, "I know that. But I make such a good living at it for what is very little effort."

Annie remained calm and friendly, which bewildered him somewhat, "Do your parents know what you do?" she asked.

He snorted, "My Dad is never at home long enough to bother, but my Mum would kill me if she knew." His gaze dropped to the floor, the action clearly asking Annie not to tell his parents.

Annie could tell that he was a decent young man at heart; he had just got on the wrong path of life. She now felt confident to question him further. "What sort of things do you take?"

He slowly looked up, slightly afraid to make eye contact, "Cash, jewellery, laptops, that sort of thing." He said

"Obviously you keep the cash," she smiled, "but what do you do with the other stuff?"

He shrugged, still not making eye contact, "I take it over to the Council estate. You can always sell good stuff over there." He leapt to his feet, "Wait there." He had a huge beam on his face, "I'll be back in a minute, promise." Before she could say anything, he had shot out of the front door and sprinted down the road.

'Oh well', she thought, 'that's the last I shall see of him, and I so thought that I was getting through to him.'

It took Annie a few moments to get out of the chair; her old limbs weren't as supple as they used to be. She picked up the two chipped mugs and shuffled through to the kitchen to wash them. She was concerned about the young man. Ash? Was that what he said his name was? She began to reflect on how lucky she was. Not at having a youth enter her home to rob it, but that he had been a half decent lad and had not harmed her. She was just drying her hands when she heard the front door slam.

"Hello? I'm back."

As she stepped into the living room, Annie was surprised to see Ash, standing with a wide grin on his face, holding up a carrier bag. "Tea, coffee, sugar and bickies." He beamed, pointing to the bag.

She tried to protest at his gift, but he knew how proud some of these old folk could be, so he ignored her and made his way through to the kitchen. "Do you take sugar Mrs? Sorry, I don't know what your name is."

"Campbell," she called back, "Annie Campbell. One sugar please, and I hope you didn't pinch that stuff."

He allowed himself a satisfying smile as he placed the shopping onto the kitchen worktop. Okay Mrs Annie Campbell, let's see if you have any decent cups. He opened a wall cupboard and his eyes widened as he saw that it was totally empty. He checked the other cupboards, all equally empty. Looking round the kitchen, all he could see was a small kettle, and the two battered mugs from earlier. No microwave, no toaster, nothing. Hell, he thought, this poor old dear has got absolutely nothing. He decided there and then what he was going to do.

A few minutes later they were back in the two old chairs with steaming mugs of tea and a packet of chocolate digestives in front of them.

Ash picked up the biscuits and held them toward the old lady, "Tuck in," he said, wearing the widest of grins, "and yes, I did pay for them."

Annie held up a hand, refusing his offer, "What did you go and do that for?" she asked, nodding at the contents of the table.

"To say sorry."

"But I don't need them." She protested.

Ash put down the biscuits, "Of course you do," he said, "You haven't got a thing in the house."

Annie was quite offended by his remark. Who did this little so-and-so think he was? First he had invaded her home, now he was trying to invade her life. "Thanks for the thought young man," she said, struggling to her feet, "But I think it's time you left now."

Ash also stood up, "I was only trying to say sorry, and to try and help." He said. He stepped towards her, gently took her hand, and placed a roll of twenty-pound notes in it.

"What on earth-?"

"I can tell you're a proud lady," he smiled, "but at least get yourself some food or something."

"But-"

"No buts Mrs C - just do it." He spun round and bolted out of the door, and this time she knew he would not be coming back.

Annie stared at the bundle of notes in total bewilderment. Why had this lad come to rob her and then ended up giving her all this money? Why on earth did he want her to buy food?

"Hi Mum, aren't you ready yet?"

Annie looked up and saw her daughter standing in the doorway. "Oh, er, hello dear. What did you say?"

Annie's daughter stepped into the room and looked strangely at her mother, "You should be ready by now Mum. All your stuff is in the new granny flat waiting for you, and a van is on its way to collect this old rubbish for the tip before the new people move in. She saw the tea and biscuits on the tatty little table, "Been saying goodbye to the neighbours?" she said warmly.

"Something like that." Annie grinned to herself as she slipped the notes into her pocket. She looked around her, said goodbye to her old house, and left for a new life with her daughter and family.

Richard O'Callaghan was born in 1953 and is a lifelong resident of Norwich, Norfolk. He spent many years as a newsagent, but retired early due to a physical disability. An avid reader of crime fiction and mysteries, he was encouraged by his wife to begin writing his own stories. He has written a collection of short stories (unpublished), a small publication on local history, which was accepted by the local press, and is currently working on a Cri-Fi novel. Educated to A-level English, he shuns the computer until writing the final draft, preferring to use a typewriter or fountain pen. He has a wife, three grown-up sons, and a very spoilt dog.

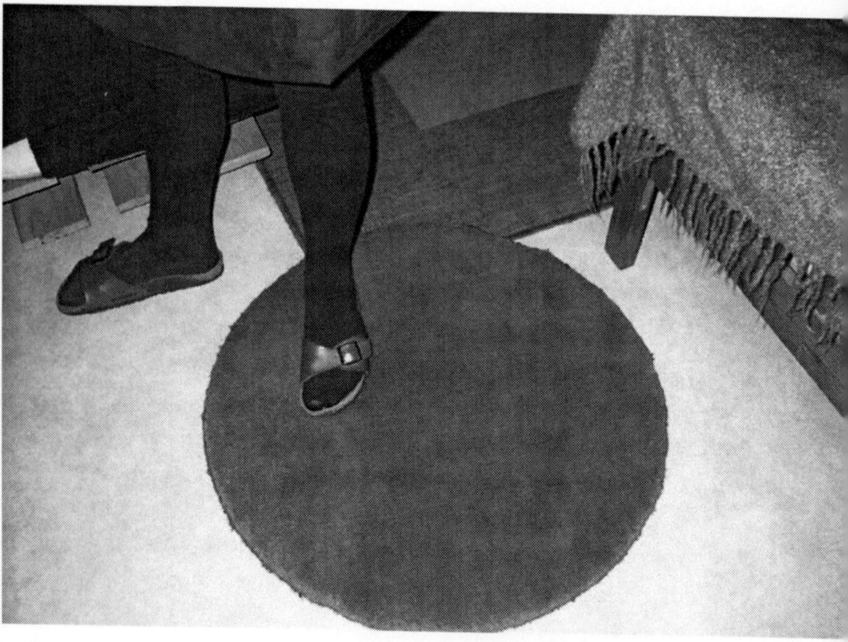

Photograph by Pierre-Jean Chignard

THE BIGGEST WHORE IN WESTBURY

NATASHA LUCAS

It started with a game of Twister. I had to put my right foot on red and my left hand on yellow, and there it was: his arm touching my boob. Not that I had much boob to touch at that point, but still, it sent a shock through my tragic denim dungarees right down to my Clarks patent leathers. It was the nineties, I was nine, what can I say?

After Twister everything changed. We stopped playing cops and robbers in the park out the back of our houses and I grew self-conscious climbing up to our tree house first. "Stop looking at my bum, you doofus!" I'd shout back down, my face aflame.

"Why you so red, pooface?" Billy would ask at the top.

"I'm hot!" I'd snap back and he'd look at me with an expression I didn't yet recognise, but over the next decade I'd see repeated on the faces of boys I was dating. "Uh-huh, honey, if you say so, dear." At nine and a half, Billy was already learning how to 'handle' me.

Being handled by Billy made me mad. Perhaps not then, in the tree, but a little later, when we started secondary school and Lee Price asked me if I wanted to be his girlfriend and Billy looked at me like I was the biggest whore in Westbury. He'd crack jokes about Lee's red hair and freckly arms as we walked home together and I'd have to say I liked those things, even though I was secretly grossed out by what Sally Smith had said about Lee growing ginger pubes.

Billy was nice when Lee dumped me, though. Took me to our tree house and gave me a whole packet of chocolate digestives he'd stolen from his kitchen. He started 'going out' with Stacey Pullman the following week, though, and was it my imagination or did they only hold hands when I was around? She lived on the same estate as us, so I didn't even get Billy to myself on our walk home. It was a torturous threesome. Eventually, I got so sick of asking Billy to hang out and being turned down because he'd promised to call Stacey, I wrote him a letter telling him how butt ugly Stacey was and how he could do way better and that I missed my friend and wanted him to dump her so we could hang out again. I posted it through his letterbox then ran back to my house to watch 'Sabrina the Teenage Witch'.

The next morning Billy turned up as usual to walk to school but Stacey was nowhere to be seen. I wanted to make some witty comment, but my mind went blank. I was actually a little afraid to step out onto the street with Billy. What did it mean that I had this much power over his love life?

My fear wasn't totally ungrounded. As soon as we reached the end of our street and turned onto

the track towards school, Billy pulled me into a gap between the hedges and stuck his tongue down my throat.

My first kiss.

I think about that kiss today, staring at Billy's picture in the paper. Did that kiss lead to this?

It felt like drowning in mashed potato. Billy tasted of toothpaste and coco-pops. His front teeth pressed so hard into my lip they left a dent. And his tongue shot inside my mouth like a soggy snake that's spotted its prey.

It was over as soon as it started and Billy straightened up and looked at me with a grin. I wanted to ask what he thought he was doing, to act all hard and punk and pretend that wasn't the most romantic thing that had happened in my thirteen and a third years on this planet. I wanted Billy to think I was cool and experienced and that he'd have to work to win over my affections.

Instead I gaped at him, growing seriously conscious of the pimple above my left eyebrow.

Billy broke the silence. "So you gonna be my girlfriend or what?"

And that was it. I couldn't think of a 'what', so with a literally stolen kiss I became Billy's girlfriend. We held hands walking to and from school and each night we met in the tree house to press our slimy tongues together. Neither of us knew what we were doing, so our kisses never progressed beyond the wet fish stage, but Billy did learn in time to keep his teeth away from my lips.

Within a week it went around the school that

Billy and I had *done it*, despite my protestations that all we'd done was kiss. In hindsight, it was probably Billy that started the rumour. Acting all chivalrous, though, he told me that, to protect my honour, we should pretend not to be together at school. So we stopped talking during breaks and sat apart in Maths. We went out for almost four years, but each lunchtime I sat with my girlfriends watching across the quad as Billy flirted with the 'popular' girls and ate lunch with boys who teased me.

"I have to make them think I'm single," he explained on the way home. "If I didn't flirt, they'd know something was up. It's all to protect you, babe. You don't want those skank rumours going around again, do you?"

I never asked him why people would think I was a skank if they knew we were officially girlfriend and boyfriend. Weren't skanks the ones who made out with boys they *weren't* going out with? I never told Billy that seeing him flirt with other girls made me cry in my room at night. I never told him my mum thought he was 'trouble' or my friends suspected I'd made our whole relationship up.

Instead, I told myself it didn't matter what other people thought; what mattered was that we were in love and the world stood still when we climbed into our tree house.

The summer following our first kiss that tree house underwent quite the transformation. No longer was it the place Billy and I had played

spies or pirates or Mighty-Morphing Power Rangers. No longer did I look for our scratched initials in the bark and think of the afternoon we'd pretended to become blood brothers, but been too scared to cut ourselves so settled for holding hands and swearing a solemn oath to always protect each other from robots and vampires and Gary Lendall, the chubby loner kid who chased us out of the park saying he'd eat us.

No, that summer the tree house became somewhere very different. For a start, Billy found some old curtains of his mum's in their shed and pinned them to the branches around the rotting platform. "For privacy," he told me. It was mostly dry that summer but as soon as autumn hit, those curtains grew the ugliest mould I've still ever seen.

The first time Billy took my top off I could smell his shampoo and the cut grass of the field beneath us. "Go on, let me," he'd been begging for weeks. I'd slapped his hand down each time and told him I was shy. I'd been examining myself in the mirror and decided my left boob was significantly smaller than my right. I'd sheepishly asked my mum if this was normal while she was doing the ironing, but she'd snapped: "Why? Who are you thinking of showing them to?"

Too scared to broach the subject with anyone else, I'd decided to take matters into my own hands. Hoping gravity would do its job, I taught myself to sleep on my left rather than my right side. After three weeks of pornographic dreams

and slumber interrupted by a panicked need to rearrange myself into my natural boob-job pose, I was convinced I could see results.

So, on the second Wednesday of the holidays, I told Billy he could do it. Smiling so I could see his teeth, he tore my Disneyland Paris T-shirt over my head, yanking my arm practically out of its socket and feasted his eyes on my tiny titties. Dumbly, I'd thought a look would be enough. I'd thought I'd give him what he'd been asking for and we'd live happily ever after. But with a hunger in his eyes, he leapt on me and we struggled on the hard tree house floor, rolling way too close to the edge as he ran his rough hands over my breasts and rubbed the crotch of his jeans into my leg.

I was terrified. I could feel him. We'd done sex education. I knew what an erection was. I'd even seen a picture of a penis. But it had been in a textbook and it had belonged to a man, a big hairy adult man. I couldn't imagine Billy, my sweet, blonde-haired, goofy grinning Billy having one of *those*.

But there it was, rubbing against my leg. And here Billy was, lying on top of me, crushing my rib cage, one hand pinching my nipple way too hard and the other reaching down beyond my belly button, tugging at my cutoffs.

"What are you doing?" I finally spoke out, channelling the voice of a thousand women and a thousand more who have never found that voice.

"You're so hot, baby!" Billy whispered into my

ear and a detached part of myself thought he didn't sound like Billy at all, he sounded like some sleazebag trying to seduce Jen on Dawson's Creek. I thought about myself as Jen and smiled, thinking Dawson was probably about to climb the trunk and save me, punch Billy on the nose and send him spiralling out of the tree, then hand me my shirt and turn around while I put it on.

Then I looked at Billy and remembered he was my Dawson. He was the boy I was madly in love with. He was the boy who treated me like a princess.

"Can we take things slow?" I asked nervously, hoping Billy wouldn't hate me.

"Sure, sure, baby, whatever you want," whispered Billy, still rubbing up against me, but complying by placing both hands firmly on my breasts.

I went home that night with a splinter in my back and an icky feeling in my belly.

Billy and I spent all summer going back and forth. He'd get all hot and heavy and tell me how beautiful I was, how much he wanted me, and I'd feel guilty for saying no each time. I gave in bit by bit. First he was allowed to unbutton my shorts but not go beneath my knickers. Then I agreed to do the same for him. I touched his penis on August 22nd. It felt like nothing I'd touched before. It was hot and smooth and made my hand smell afterwards.

The first time he got it out of his pants he thrust it straight into my mouth with no warning and

I gagged so hard tears came to my eyes. But he told me that's what girls were meant to do if they weren't ready for sex. That experience and Billy's crude explanation no doubt sped up my 'readiness'.

Billy and I had sex on the last day before school. I was fourteen and one month. He was fourteen and seven months. The curtains were beginning to smell and we could hear the kids playing on the swings at the other end of the field. It hurt worse than getting hit in the shin with a hockey ball and having to sit out the rest of the match. We used a condom; we'd sat through videos of volcanic vaginas and crusty cocks at school. That, at least, is a relief.

The next day the kids in my class gave me funny looks and my girl friends refused to sit with me. I asked Billy if he'd told anyone and he said, "No way, babe, I have too much respect for you. But if people are talking maybe we should be more careful. Perhaps we shouldn't walk to school together."

So for the next week I had to walk behind Billy while he walked with that slutbag Stacey and she laughed at all his jokes. After that I started leaving later and getting in trouble at registration. I didn't care. Billy and I still met in the tree house each night after our teas. I spent all day looking forward to those meetings, imagining myself a Juliet to his Romeo, pretending the evils the other kids shot me didn't register. I was too sophisticated to care what they thought. They were kids; I was now a woman.

In reality, though, our evening trysts involved Billy dictating I strip, get into whichever pornographic position he and his mates had sniggered about that day, banging the shit out of me for approximately thirty-five seconds, then chucking the condom into the hedges and letting me walk home alone.

It wasn't until I got to university and learnt about feminism and women's rights and (my god!) the female orgasm, that I realised there was anything wrong with me and Billy. The first time a guy was nice to me in bed I broke down in tears. For that matter, the first time I had sex in an actual bed I broke down in tears.

After two months of dating Phil and one month of crying each time we made love, he gently suggested I make an appointment with the campus counsellor. I joined a waiting list and eventually became one of those people unzipping their skin for a stranger in weekly one-hour sessions.

I had so much anger. It came as a surprise. I'd never felt angry at Billy when we were teenagers, but here I was raging once a week at an MC Escher print on a magnolia wall.

"Perhaps you should confront Billy, tell him how you feel," my comfortingly homely counsellor suggested.

So I did. I travelled home and knocked on his door, asked his mum if he was in. She looked at me with suspicion, but told me he'd left for work, he'd be back at six. I returned and we took

a walk around the park. He wanted to go up to the tree house, see what was left, but I refused. I tried to tell him how I felt, how he'd used me, the damage he'd done. He laughed. He actually laughed. The boy I'd promised to protect from vampires and robots and Gary Lendall laughed in my face and told me I'd 'loved it'.

I returned to uni more furious than ever. Phil broke up with me, said I had 'unresolved emotional issues'. I put my head down, stayed in counselling, graduated with a 2-1. I eventually found a boy I didn't feel the need to cry with. I slowly rebuilt my idea of the world. I slowly convinced myself that none of it was my fault. That even if I did choose the yellow spot that stretched my body over Billy's shoulder, that even if all those years ago I secretly wanted his nine-year-old arm to touch my nonexistent breast, I didn't ask to be treated that way. I was not responsible for that.

But today I wonder, am I responsible for this? For Billy sexually assaulting a nineteen-year-old outside a club last Saturday? For, according to her mates, plying her with drinks and dragging her down an alley when she said she didn't want to go home with him? Did I teach him those actions? By not saying no, was I silently letting my sex down, inadvertently reinforcing his behaviour?

I feel sick looking at this article. Why now? I wonder selfishly. Why, just as I'm finally stepping into my future, must I be dragged back into the past? Has Billy been doing stuff like this all

along and only just got caught? Was I simply the first of a string of women he broke and left to rebuild themselves in a world that calls them whores?

I force myself to reread the story. I feel sorry for the girl, already being blamed by the newspaper: drunk, short skirt, excessive drinking – these are the words the journalist highlights. They're the sisters of the words I've been afraid of all my life. Every time I've told someone I've waited for them to turn away in disgust, to tell me I let it happen, I encouraged him, that it wasn't that big a deal, that he was just a kid; that, like Billy said, I must have 'loved' it.

I want to tell this girl I'm sorry, I know how she feels. But maybe I don't. Even drunk and wearing what she was, this girl found the strength to say no. Even now, after that, strength did her no good; she's found more to press charges, to face the media and the insults. She's fighting in the way I never did, perhaps never could.

We need more women like her, I think, turning the page and stroking my swollen belly.

Natasha Lucas is a part-time barista and full-time writer who wears the word 'feminist' on her sleeve. She has published stories and nonfiction essays in Ducts, The Wanderlust Review, Duality, Brand, Underwired, Foreign Flavours and Inside Out. She is currently seeking representation for her memoir and her novel and doodling ideas for her next project.

Photograph by Sean Lotman

DISTANCE

MICHELLE TUDOR

Ito sat on a local train and rested his head back against the window. From that angle he could just about see the scenery through the window opposite him; it appeared as if from the tip of his nose. The winter sky and blanket of snow over the fields formed one huge white sheet that wrapped around the train, the only indication of separation between the sky and the ground was a few houses scattered messily. A sharp gust of wind blew through the rickety old carriage and he pulled his thick jacket closer and his hat further down over his ears. An old black leather diary lay on his lap and he caressed it with his icy fingertips. Next to him sat a woman, her tiny head bobbing down and then up again as she tried to fight the sleep that was overwhelming her.

Ito had been feeling old, the chills ran through his bones and he felt older than he ever had. He was nearing sixty, yet he felt as though he'd already lived sixty lives. He thought about the small warm hands of a woman from long ago, the woman he was on his way to see. "She probably won't remember you," a young woman had told him.

Three days ago he'd received a call in the late afternoon, just as he was making himself some tea; the shrill rings cut through the quiet apartment. He now sat on the long journey northwards; it was the wrong time of year to be leaving the warm crowds of the city to a village deep in the countryside, where the snow and cold got into your bones. A village that was much like the one he had grown up in with the woman, their youth existing in a bubble now, forever intrinsically linked. Ito never remembered his hometown without her in it. They'd left those deep winters behind them long ago, but the shivers that he felt brought back the feelings that still remained inside of him. He remembered how they'd sit on the front step of her house after school every day and talk about the same things over and over again.

"Ito, why am I this me - why can't I be another version of myself?" She'd asked him once.

"Maybe you can," he'd said.

"Not here I can't," she'd replied as she looked up at the sky.

"You can be whoever you want to be, cut your hair, start wearing different clothes…" he'd wanted to continue but she'd interrupted him.

"That's not changing me though, it's not inside." She looked at him and then down at the floor, one single tear drop fell into the vast white powder. She'd carved their names into the snow that night – *Misaki and Ito* – and he'd wanted her to draw a heart around it, but she didn't.

He used to think of those moments often but as he got older, the thoughts of his youth and the chance of his seeing her again faded. He replayed the snowy night over and over again, and the day she left with her parents for another city, he waved at her and she put her hand to the window and four hundred miles drove a wedge between them.

He wondered how she'd changed, if she'd ever become another her.

He arrived in the town at four in the afternoon as the winter sun was beginning to set. He walked from the small train station seeing only a handful of people along the way, he could see them through the low windows of the houses, huddled together in front of heaters and covered in blankets. The falling snow was difficult to wade through and it felt as though he'd jumped head first into an ice cold lake, emptying his lungs of air. By the time he reached the small nursing home, Ito was panting heavily and glad to feel the rush of warm air that hit him as soon as he stepped through the glass doors towards the small desk.

"Can I help?" One of the nurses behind the desk asked.

"Ito... my name is Ito," he replied trying to catch his breath.

They looked at him blankly for a few seconds until a woman that had entered behind him walked towards the desk. Ito looked at her, a feeling of familiarity washed over him but he couldn't distinguish where he knew the dark-haired woman from. The woman's presence seemed to alight something in the woman behind the desk who suddenly broke into a smile.

"Ahhh," she said nodding at the other woman.

"You must have had quite a journey," the other desk clerk said.

"Yes..." Ito began, but the two women started talking to the woman who appeared at his side, so he wandered around the reception. Gentle flute music was playing somewhere down the hall, so he walked towards it. He looked at the doors as he passed them, wondering which one belonged to Misaki. He began to remember how she'd looked the last time he saw her, long black hair draped over her face, her slightly crooked-toothed smile and the sweet perfume that perfectly captured the essence of a seventeen-year-old girl.

Ito peeked his head into a few of the rooms with open doors, in one of them a man sat staring out of the window at a ginger cat, in another a woman was being fed by an overweight nurse. He walked on until he reached a large room at the end, the room was bathed in an early-evening haze and a woman sat at the huge glass windows staring at the falling snow which could just be seen in the failing light.

When he reached her, he looked into her faded eyes and was convinced it could be no-one else but Misaki. She was a tiny fraction of a woman and her once long hair had been chopped into small spikes that stuck up in different directions. She sat staring out of the window and he could barely hear her breathing.

"Misaki?" Ito whispered.

There was no response from the woman but he sat down in front of her. Distant feelings washed over him and his eyes started to well up, he wanted to touch her hand but he suddenly became frozen in his seat. He willed his mouth to move.

"Misaki… it's me Ito." He tried again.

He thought he saw the tiniest of flickers in her eyes, like wisps of ash floating up into the air from a bonfire.

"I've waited so long to see you…" he put his hands together. "Do you remember me?" He spoke softly but she stayed silent.

"I've come all the way from Tokyo to see you…" he shuddered. "It's so cold here, I don't know how you stand it. I still remember the night of that rainstorm when our street got flooded, we thought the world was going to wash away there was so much, do you remember? You said one day you'd move to Hawaii and study on the beach." He looked at her sad eyes and her pale hands, she looked so cold.

Ito traced his fingers over the black diary he was still carrying. "I used to keep everything in here," his eyes trailed over the ridges. "When you left I stapled in the letters you sent to me, since that last one I never opened it again. I promised myself I'd wait until I saw you again." Ito took off his coat and got himself comfortable in the window seat.

"Shall I read some to you?" He didn't wait for her silent answer.

The leather creaked as he slipped off the rubber band, so many years he'd held onto it, waiting for the moment he could share those memories with her again. As he opened the cover slowly, a small photograph slipped out a little. He smiled to himself.

"I'd forgotten about this," he said looking at the crumbling photograph in his hand, aged and decaying, much like he felt. Attached to the back with a rusty staple was a letter, yellow and musty, like an unclean bathroom in an abandoned house. Ito recognised the familiar curves of the handwriting, yet the words it formed were a distant memory. As he read them he tried to piece together the place it described; the old playground in the old town, back then newly installed, the slide shining silver in the sunshine, enticing them. He imagined it had red stairs, although he didn't know if the memory was correct. He did remember the tree in the picture though, the grand old tree in the centre of the park, carved with initials of children past, like gravestone etchings, most of them long gone. The letter described a kiss in childish glee, it informed him it was "soft, slow and ticklish" but he couldn't bring that back no matter how hard he tried, he couldn't feel it anymore. Almost forty years gone

in an instant, memories fading more every day, his mind a series of fragments of what had and what might have been. His own failed engagement, the last letter when Misaki had confessed that she'd never wanted to be a housewife.

Ito was broken from his thoughts by a small boy who ran into the room, he was about five with raven black hair and he was chewing loudly. He could see that the boy had run from his mother who was down the corridor talking to one of the nurses.

"Graaam…" he screeched through a mouthful of rice-cake.

Ito suddenly realised how little he knew of Misaki's life since he'd last seen her. Ito looked at the boy.

"Hello," he said.

"Hello," he repeated spraying crumbs on the floor.

"What's your name?" Ito asked him but the boy had walked over to him and was staring at the diary on his lap. He looked up at Ito.

"How old are you?" Ito tried again.

"How old are you?" The boy repeated laughing to himself.

Ito chuckled "Older than you but younger than the Cherry Tree outside." The boy giggled and ran back out of the door he came through.

Ito looked back at Misaki who hadn't moved at all since he'd sat down. He began to flick through the diary again, searching for images in his mind to back up the words. He sighed heavily when they wouldn't come.

"What happened Misaki? Why did you stop writing?" He pleaded even though he knew she wouldn't answer, not now, maybe not ever.

"Do you remember the last words you wrote, shall I read them?" He questioned her fervently.

"You'd told me about your mother's new job at the government office and then you said…" Ito looked to the end of the letter. "He left me in January, I think perhaps he couldn't stand the idea of a new year with me." A wave of sadness rushed over Ito, he hated to think of her so unhappy. He pictured her sitting on a bench under a plum blossom tree, he knew it was his own memory of when they were younger because he'd never even seen her new house, but every time he'd thought of her it was under that tree, alone and scared.

"I'm sorry Misaki… I wish I'd tried to find you."

Ito sat in silence for a long while, caressing the diary and staring at Misaki and then out at the snow. The feeling of familiarity existed and hugged him tightly. His heart felt heavy at never getting the chance to hear her speak again and to never make new memories with her.

The sound of a horn followed by a short, sharp tune brought him out of his thoughts and when he looked up, he couldn't believe his eyes. Making its way down the small street in front of the home was a familiar grey potato truck. Ito could smell the sweetness before it even got close to the window and was suddenly thrown back to their youth – Misaki's grandfather had owned a sweet potato truck and the familiar jingle and the warmth of the small stone heater in the back made them jump up from whatever they were doing and run to him as fast as their seven-year-old legs would carry them. Back here and now he moved with less agility, his back creaking as he turned to look on.

As he closed his eyes and leant back against the window, he heard the two women at the desk down the hall. "Be careful not to wander off the paths, you'd be lost forever in the snowy hills." They both giggled.

Ito stayed there for a few more moments and when he looked back at Misaki, he saw that her eyes were closed, they were both so tired now.

"I know how you feel." He said quietly.

He moved closer to her and whispered "I'm going to stay here Misaki, I'll stay with you, I'm sorry I didn't find you sooner… but I'll stay now, I won't let us be separated again, I promise." He smiled at her as she sighed in her sleep.

Ito heard a small cough and when he looked up and saw the dark-haired woman who had followed him into the home, she was looking at them both, with a small smile she made her way over the window and sat next to him.

"How are you feeling Ito?" She said.

"I'm fine… can I stay and talk to Misaki a while longer?" Ito said, suddenly remembering the woman as the one sitting next to him on the train. He looked at her and she gave him another smile and patted his hand gently.

"Your room is ready." She said and Ito stared at her.

A moment later one of the women from the desk came in and began to wheel Misaki out of the room, Ito began to protest but the woman put her hand on his arm.

"Nao has to go back to her room," the woman smiled and Ito's mind swirled, he looked around forgetting where he was for a split second, he began to panic and the telephone that rang in the background cut through his brain like a bullet train on rusty tracks.

He looked up at the woman, "Misaki… her name is Misaki."

WONDERFUL WORLD

ANTONIO CRUZ

"Welcome to the Wacky Menagerie of Marvelous Marvels!" The guide threw his arms up in a dramatic display. His striped, neon top hat almost flew off his head with the slight breeze. Clancy was sure that he had seen the man before. Not in the ridiculous, multicolored three-piece suit and clown paint he wore now, but in a more "normal" look. It reminded him of his dad when he would dress as Santa Claus.

"Who is this guy?" Kat, his best friend, raised an eyebrow.

The guide spun around. "In due time." He held out a white-gloved hand. Kat shook it as if it was solidified anthrax.

They stood on a hill. The grass should have been a lush green; instead it looked unnaturally bright to Clancy. Clouds swirled in a purple sky.

At the bottom of the hill was a circus tent. It was large and covered the lot it was erected over. Sharp, orange swirls moved over the white canvas like they were alive. They looked like slivers of water sliding down a window.

"What is so marvelous about this menagerie?"

The peculiar guide began to sing and skip down the hill. He flew dangerously high but always landed safe before bouncing again. "Over the hill, through no woods, to our wonderland we go..." he continued with his ridiculous song.

Clancy and Kat gave each other a look and stumbled down the hill.

They got to the bottom and landed with a thud on the concrete. It seemed to vibrate beneath them as it absorbed the shock of their teenage bodies.

The guide stood next to a door. His hands were folded behind him. The entire time he would not look at Clancy directly, only giving him shuffling glances.

"Do we dare venture in?" His voice was playful.

"First," Kat said while shoving her black curls from her eyes, "Who are you? What's your name?"

He looked to the sky. For a moment the unstable glee left his face, as if he was remembering a long-forgotten memory. "I am me and you are we and that is me," he looked down to Kat, "I am Gatherer."

"But please call me Gabber. Gatherer is my business name." He swung around and entered the tent. The door shut quickly behind him.

"Should we go?" Clancy looked unsure.

"How did we get here?"

"Last thing I remember we were driving on the back roads."

"Maybe," Kat said, "this is a dream."

Clancy looked to the door. There was a white sign on it and it looked like it would be an emergency exit door. Instead it said "PLEASE, DO

ENTER." He wanted to know why he felt he already knew Gabber. "Only one way to find out." Clancy swung the door open. It was metal, ordinary, and out of place. They went in.

They were anticipating darkness, a dim hole of stinking animals. But the shelter shone brighter than the outside. It was like a cloudless summer day. The source of the brilliant light was unknown. Clancy could not find any light fixtures.

The two found themselves in the din of a crowd. It seemed to them to be a festival or marketplace. Shops and stands lined the walls. Even inside they could see the orange swirls dance along the tent.

Gabber could not be picked from the crowd. Everyone was dressed in a fashion similar to him. Clancy and Kat became very aware of their jeans and T-shirts.

"Oi! You two," the tender of the nearest shop came wobbling over. His great belly sloshed in front of him, and his overalls alternated between bright and dim like a lightening bug.

"You two look a bit," he scratched at his chin grizzle, "out of place."

"We came with Gabber."

His chuckle was hard and full. "Of course you did." He pointed a chubby finger to the other side of the market. "Gabber went that way. He didn't forget about you both. Gabber is always seen when he wants to."

Clancy looked around the merchant to get a look at his stand. Golden streamers were hung around a sign that read "Howard's Razzles and

Dazzles." The streamers continuously spun like a chain on a moving bike.

All the hangers and hooks of his shop were empty.

"Did everybody buy your things?"

"Huh?" Howard looked back to his shop. Then he laughed his large laugh and wheeled back around. "Buy! With money! I forgot how peculiar you people can be." He walked back to his stand shaking his head and laughing all the time.

"That was weird." The two friends walked through the center of the market. Everyone let them through without a fuss, a polite crowd despite how packed in they were. The ground continued to shimmer with each step, like small rocks being dropped into a pond.

Clancy looked around. All the shops appeared to carry nothing, just like Howard's. Some of the shoppers held out their hands as if they were holding things. Shopkeepers smiled and bobbed their heads enthusiastically like salesmen.

"I'm as confused as you." Kat said.

They turned the corner, leaving the market. The next sight was, once again, unexpected.

The tent continued to surprise. They had never seen a grander arena, and they were at its very top. The stadium was in the shape of a bowl. The bottom of the bowl was hundreds of rows down. Its seats were not made of cheap plastic and cramped together, they were all red plush thrones, fit for royalty and spread out comfortably.

Gabber was in the middle of the empty ring at the bottom. Its field seemed to be made of grass, but he glided across it effortlessly. He motioned for them to walk down as he did laps.

The walk down was slow. "Is there going to be a show?" Clancy asked as they approached.

"Oh, yes. There will be quite the show." Gabber stopped his skating and held onto the enclosure. He motioned for his two visitors to sit in two front seats.

The seats were as comfortable as they looked. Clancy sunk into the chair slowly like a familiar bed. Golden trim shimmered on the seats, and it felt like glass when he ran his fingers along it.

"How are you doing that?" Kat asked.

"Doing what? Standing?" Gabber was serious.

"No, when you were skating. It looks like you're on grass."

"That's because I am." He raised a foot high enough for the visitors, "I am grass-skating."

It looked to Clancy as if Gabber was only wearing bright clown shoes. He shrugged it off. "Gabber, what's a Razzle? Or a Dazzle?"

"You must have met Howard. Wonderful guy. Smart, too. The key to his shop is that he offers only a little Razzle-Dazzle at a time. You never hear anybody say 'all I want is a bunch of Razzle-Dazzle'. That would be chaos. It is always a *little* Razzle-Dazzle. Know what I am saying?"

Clancy shook his head.

"Excellent," Gabber slapped his hands together. "I must begin my preparations. Everyone will be here in seconds." He shook hands with Clancy and Kat. He still avoided eye contact with Clancy.

He trotted away comically with his long limbs flailing, to an exit on the opposite side of the arena.

The two didn't see the need for such a quick exit. They both looked behind their chairs to see if anybody was coming.

All the spectators were there, whispering excitedly, when they were not there just a moment before. "What the…" when they turned back around the other side was just as suddenly full.

Kat looked at Clancy. The excitement of the moment danced in her eyes. "Could this be real?" She reached across Clancy's chair and went for his hand. The bright light was dimming. He saw what she was going for and adjusted nervously. Her hand fell to the side of her chair.

The lights were dark. A spotlight landed on the tunnel on the far side. There was the beat of a drum roll at a much higher pitch. Kat recognized the sound. "I guess that would be a flute roll." Clancy nodded.

The crowd around them stomped their feet to the beat of the flutes. Clancy and Kat followed suit but were stuck off-time.

"Beings and other beings," Gabber's voice boomed through the arena, "welcome to the Wacky Menagerie Show of Marvelous Marvels." He walked to the middle of the ring. "First." Everybody fell silent immediately. "A song."

A hidden band broke into a tune that neither of the visitors had heard the likes of. Clancy could hear electric guitars, fiddles, accordions, mandolins, and sitars. Kat heard banjos, ukuleles, oboes, flutes, and cellos. The sound was upbeat and dominating.

Dancers poured from the tunnel like bubbles from a wand, in two lines sidestepping. They wore purple jumpsuits with yellow hats, twirled poles that changed colors with every spin.

Elephants the size of ponies followed. They would stand on their hind legs and walk before falling back on all fours again. Monkeys on pogo sticks wearing tiny fezzes followed.

The dancers, the crowd, and Gabber all sang with a practiced precision:

Magnificent Marvels
Magnificent Marvels
We are all Magnificent Marvels
We sing, we dance, we cry
We are just imperfect all of the time
Magnificent Marvels
Magnificent Marvels
We lived, we tried, we died
Now we have fun all of the time
Magnificent Marvels
Magnificent Marvels
We are all Magnificent Marvels

And so on. Clancy and Kat only caught the first few measures. After all, there was a lot going on for them.

The dancers sidestepped around the outside of the ring, two cogs ever turning in opposite directions. The elephants two-hopped across the middle of the ring, while the monkeys pogo-sticked around. Gabber was raised into the air by a pillar that emerged from the ground. He waved and turned, wave and turned, until everyone in the crowd was greeted as the song and dance went on below.

Kat, with a smiling face, looked over at Clancy. His left leg shook up and down at a rapid pace. He looked to her and gave a crooked smile. "Isn't this great?" she yelled. He looked at her and she saw fear in his eyes. The man next to him nodded gleefully at her question.

It started with the horns and ended with the strings. The song began to slow itself, ease into an ending. Gabber conducted with sticks from his pillar in the sky. The song ended abruptly. Everyone stood up with an ovation. Everyone except for Clancy.

The pillar lowered and Gabber stepped off. The ovation had ended after several bows, and the clapping stopped as quickly as the song. When Kat looked around, everyone had disappeared again.

With a spring in his step, Gabber returned to his guests. "And so ends Act I. What did you think?"

"Fantastic, brilliant, and unreal." Kat smiled, ear to ear.

"Ridiculous. Pointless. Where's the struggle? The conflict? It is just fluff." Clancy crossed his arms and slouched in his chair.

A shadow fell across Gabber as he looked down. "What are you upset about, Clancy?"

For the first time the guide looked directly at

Clancy. He had not said his name before, and as soon as he had, Clancy knew the voice, pinpointed it firmly in his past.

Behind the multicolored make up, underneath the ridiculous hat, Clancy was looking into the eyes of his brother. He had been dead for a decade.

"This can't be real. It can't be you. It's not you, Rob. You got sick, you-"

"Died. I know." He said. "My name is Gabber now. And I am your guide."

"Guide to what? This isn't real." Clancy said. Kat continued to smile.

"You are far from the first person to deny its existence, Clancy. And that is what makes it so wonderful." Gabber's giddy spirit returned. He pulled out his two conductors sticks and walked away. "Time for Act Two."

The happily ravenous crowd appeared again. Kat's excitement matched theirs. Clancy continued to brood. As he looked around he noticed a difference in the audience. Youthful, manly faces became harder and more grizzled, like weathered sea rock. The women's faces were softer and rounder and wore humble make up. His own hands began to feel course upon the plush chair.

The flute roll returned and the preposterous band played again. Its beat continued at the same raucous pace, but Clancy heard something more to it the second time around. It was found in the backbeat, underneath the pomp and frill of the louder instruments. He isolated it in the heavy strings, the cellos and the double basses. They were playing something slower, more somber.

Gabber, from his pillar tower, used his sticks like he was a controller on the runway, shoving them from his front to his back.

From the tunnel, the sidestepping dancers returned. Their clothes were darker, the stripes less wild, the shades of color more tame. The poles that danced in their hands flashed lazier than before.

Creatures that hopped on four legs joined the prancing elephant ponies and the pogo monkeys. There were four of them and they were painted like zebras. It was a wonder to the visitors that their legs did not buckle under them. There was a sharp horn, as white and as hard as marble, sticking from their heads.

A new song sprung:

Magnificent Marvels
Magnificent Marvels
We all were Magnificent Marvels
We sang, we danced, we tried
And I just miss it all the time
Magnificent Marvels
Magnificent Marvels
We live, we tried, we died
How I wish I learned to stay alive
Magnificent Marvels
Magnificent Marvels
We all were Magnificent Marvels

Clancy looked to Kat. She was yelling and clapping without a worry in the world. But he only recognized her by laugh. Something had changed with the act. Her hair looked thinner, the curls were less emphatic. There were lines at the edges of her mouth and eyes. They were turned upwards, a life used to smiling. But she was supposed to only be seventeen.

He felt his own face. It was rough. Hard lines were present when before he had none. "Kat, do you feel odd?"

"Why are you looking at me like that? Just enjoy the show."

Monkeys leaped from their pogo-sticks and landed on the backs of the hopping zebras. They broke through the lines of dancers. This created a chaos within the ring. The dancers broke ranks and sidestepped where they pleased. Elephants kicked at whoever ran past. Horns were being swept side to side, knocking around whoever got in the way.

The band ceased. Gabber slid down the pillar. Clancy thought it could have been as tall as ten stories. Gabber landed cleanly on the back of a waiting elephant. He took it by the ears and led the crazed procession back from where they came to the roar of a standing ovation.

"How was that?" The visitors jumped as a voice broke the sudden silence that fell in the great arena. They looked behind and it was Gabber, legs-crossed, lounging in a chair.

Kat's jaw was slack in admiration. Clancy looked at her and saw gray streaks sprouting from the top of her head. "How did you-"

"There are a lot of things you may find surprising about here. About me."

His brother was not convinced. "This is still not real."

Gabber sighed long and heavy. He hummed to himself and looked to find an answer in the great empty place. "You are not long for this place. I missed you and it was good to see you. Being your big brother meant a lot to me. Only wished it was longer."

Clancy found it hard to talk. But he knew he needed to say what he wanted to. "You were a good brother."

Gabber only nodded with eyes closed. "What is the last thing you remember before coming to this place?"

He remembered his work-in-progress muscle car, jumping up and down, the suspension pushed to its limits. "The road was too much for the car. It felt like we were flying. Kat was being launched from her seat."

Kat still held the same expression. She was frozen and did not seem to notice the conversation of the two brothers.

"Kid, I just wanted to see you. And talk to you. Your only reaction, naturally, would be rejection. That is because it is not your turn to believe."

Clancy brought his hand back to his face. It felt smooth again. "I want to believe."

"Do not tempt me. Your will to live must stay strong. It is not your time. You are to live a long and happy life." Gabber stood up. His knees cracked and Clancy saw the human behind the act. "Don't worry about Kat," Gabber said, "she will be safe and happy here."

"It is time for Act Three," Gabber climbed over the barricade and looked back, "you will not be here much longer. This isn't goodbye, Clancy. I will see you again."

"Rob, wait-"

"The show must go on." He did not look back. He stopped in the middle of the ring. The pillar did not raise and his head remained down.

"This is just splendid," Kat woke from her catatonic state, "isn't life just great?"

"This isn't life, Kat. It is something else."

"You got that right."

He looked around and noticed the crowd had returned again. This time they stayed silent. They were aged dramatically and looked tired. Clancy looked to Kat. The curls in her hair were back. They were white like cotton. Not everyone gets to die old. "It isn't necessarily a tragedy," he said.

The menagerie featured no animals in the last act. In rows of four the dancers came out walking slow with feet pointed in opposite directions. Their elbows were bent and their hands were outstretched, palms up. The movements reminded Clancy of when he used to pretend to be an Egyptian on the playground.

He was sure they were people or, perhaps, people at one time. Their bright outfits were replaced with skin-tight black ones. They looked like walking x-rays, their bodies somehow exposed, a blue-hue highlighting the moving joints. They reminded Clancy of the year he went as a skeleton for Halloween, only so much more real.

The skeletons formed around Gabber, who continued to stand still. They held their poses, shook their hands from back and forth, and their heads swung around and around like on a swivel.

They sang:

This is Wonderful World
Wonderful World
A World of Wonder to be a part of
A Wonderful World to be
Won't you come?
Won't you come?
You'll struggle no more
No longer feel sore
A truly wonderful, wonderful world

Clancy looked at Kat. She was lost in the music. A smile was fixed on her face. His chest hurt to think of what happened.

The dancers began to pull people from the crowd into the ring. They were heading to the Kat and Clancy's side. "I hope they pick me," Kat said star-struck.

A dancer arrived and held out a bony hand to Kat. She took it and climbed over the barricade. She looked to Clancy. "Are you coming?"

The notion to grab her hand, to be pulled in with her, was being processed in his head. He thought of the hardships of life he would have to face if he left. Pain, disappointment, death, and heartache were guaranteed. So were triumph, happiness, and love. There was that.

Clancy gave Kat a last look, and felt a tinge of envy. He stood up and then headed for the exit.

Antonio Cruz is an author in his infancy. Graduating with a Creative Writing degree from University of Wisconsin-Milwaukee in December, it was only then did he find the courage to start offering his work to the world's eye. Humor is his first defensive mechanism, and he is not sure what he is hiding from just yet. His stories contain magical realism, humanism, and absurdity. You can find his semi-regular updates at theantoniocruz.wordpress.com. Antonio Cruz lives in Milwaukee WI, with his girlfriend, Jessica, and their family of cats.

Photograph by Michel Nguie

MADWOMAN STORY

Erato Ioannou - Moustaka

The tall towers of the power station soar over her in the semidarkness. For some reason that she cannot determine, she feels in tune with the environment—no longer a misfit. She listens to the waves thrashing on the pointy rocks below, to the buzzing of the power station pumping electricity into the veins of the world, to the whispers of the night. There is some strange, cool harmony in the music of it all.

They are alike—her and the dark sea. She inhales her salty perfume that carries with it stories of tales untold and forever to be held in her dark depths. Her gaze travels where the surf meets the shore, coming together as lovers' souls merging into one another, becoming one for a brief moment and then separating again, leaving behind the devastation of their abrupt and short lovemaking.

She sits on the edge of the cliff—her legs dangling as though she is sitting on a swing, like a little girl.

My daughter loves the water. She takes long bubbly baths, runs into the rain until soaking wet, and jumps into the sea with her shoes still on. I don't know what it is. If these were taken away from her, she would dry up and die like a fish in the net. That's why I don't get upset at her and let her do as she pleases. I tell her stories of mermaids living into the depths of the vast oceans, falling in love in underwater fairy tales, riding seahorses in the cool silent blueness, with pearls and sparkling seashells decorating their hair.

When I'm sad, she puts her tiny index fingers on the corners of my mouth and pushes them high into my cheeks. When I'm sad, she tells me that she wants to be like me when she grows up. She tells me that she wants to be able to write stories about mermaids. I don't necessarily believe her… I do not want her to be like me. That's my only wish.

My daughter doesn't know my friend—the madwoman. I'm not going to let her anywhere near her. Ever!

This madwoman friend of mine lives in the attic of my mind. Once in a while, during the long moments of insomnia, I meet up with her. The two of us sit comfortably in the attic and have long meaningless chats about Reason. That's her only pursuit in life—Reason that is. Some other times we just sit side by side in silence, smoking and listening to each other breathe just to know we're alive.

Once upon a time, there was Reason. Concepts and notions were beautifully placed in particular boxes, lovely and shiny, gazing back at me with certainty and reassurance. And then I realized that clear-cut lines and shapes and predetermined pathways have become blurry and hazy and uncomfortably distorted. When one realizes that there are no limits any more, no definite colors, no categories, the realization is unwanted at first. At first!

A huge, dusty storage is all that is left from my disturbed mind, loaded with memories, and thoughts covered in cobwebs. I am in there—all sweaty and breathing heavily as though I have been running a marathon. Restless curls cover my face, my cheeks are flushing. I run my hands frantically over the dusty objects trying to fathom what was once clear and understandable. I am nothing but a madwoman in an attic heaving and hissing, tearing cobwebs trying to figure things out.

Once upon a time, before my daughter was born, things were much simpler. I would lay drunk on the kitchen floor and hurt myself in my peace and quiet. In the privacy and comfort of my own, my very own personal space. I would lay there, freeing the sorrows of my soul, and watch them flee from the self-inflicted wounds on my body. But not anymore.

My teacher. My lovely teacher. My beloved married teacher. He doesn't know the madwoman either. At least I don't think so. I wear long-sleeved shirts. We make love in the dark. He doesn't know of my scars—they are invisible. He has no fucking clue!

With him, there is no Reason. We just talk about words and what he tells me is that my words are just empty vessels;that they are mere strings of sounds, emitting a cacophony of emotions, unless... unless I pour my soul into them. But my soul has burst and splattered all around me, is small pools of murky water on the floor. And there is no way to suck it back into me.

Very often, lately, I have this dream: I am floating comfortably on a calm sea. I lay there effortlessly—my arms spread, as if expecting the dark starry sky to fall into them, and make love to me—right there on the surface of the lovely sea. The warm water splatters on the sides of my body, on my cheeks. The cool breeze surprises my naked abandoned self with its caresses like an uninvited skillful lover. This lover sees my scars, but doesn't talk about them.

Then, the sea opens up and swallows me. I am immersed in the dark water now, and for just a brief moment I am afraid. Just for a brief moment.

Right there in my fucking dream I see his face again—my lovely teacher's face. And then I realize that what I am most afraid of is when his words make me cry—when he tells me that he is not good for me, that I should run away. Then we kiss violently. We make love. We say cruel things to one another. We smoke a couple of cigarettes in silence. We fall asleep into each other's arms.

The madwoman doesn't approve of my relation with him and I try to reason with her—as if I need her approval. I tell her that human relations may not rest in the confines of solid characterizations, that they cannot withstand limitations and boundaries, nor can they be cemented in social norms. I tell her that they are multifaceted, and complex, and as incomprehensible as human nature itself. I put too much effort into putting my thoughts in well-chosen words making me sound like a textbook. I almost manage to convince even myself.

The madwoman shoves me away. Her feverish eyes stare at me full of hatred.

"If it were that simple I wouldn't have been in here searching," she says and her voice is coarse as though she had not spoken in ages. "I wouldn't have been looking for meaning in here like crazy."

"But you are crazy," I tell her, but not loud enough for her to hear me.

Every bit of logic has run away from me. It is lost and never to be found again—somewhere in the dark abyss of my very essence. But I can't tell the madwoman. I am afraid that she is going to kill herself. And, I'm kind of used to her and I can't let her do that. I wish my mind was a wonderful place for her.

On the kitchen floor I pray for simple-mindedness. I pray that my mind were simple and plain like a clean, scented shirt drying in the morning sun. But it is nothing like that. It is suffocating, filled with nonsense like a gigantic dumpster after the weekend.

He reads my story. The smoke from his cigarette lingers in front of his face making his features hazy. We sit in silence which is only punctuated by his dry cough and sighs of contempt. His chair squeaks under his weight.

"What the fuck is this?" he bursts at me. "What sentimental melodramatic bullshit is this?" he yells, and the echoes of his cruelty reverberate against every single molecule of my body and soul. He extinguishes his cigarette in swift neurotic moves. He holds the manuscript and shakes it to my face. "Don't you hear anything I tell you? What the fuck? This is nonsense!" The manuscript flies against the wall and every single sheet floats slowly downwards until it hits the floor.

My words escape the pages. They knock me down and tare me apart with their claws.

He makes love to me the same way—violently as though he hates me, as though he is taking vengeance. And then, I spend long moments in silence trying to figure him out, trying to decipher what is going on in his mind, but he is as unreadable and incomprehensible as Joycean prose.

As I watch him sleep, I think of him making love to his wife—caressing her, kissing her softly, his lips running smoothly on the curve of her neck. And the image is so clear and vivid as though I am right there, outside their window, staring at them as they make love, like some kind of sicko.

When my daughter takes a bath, she fills the tub with warm water and sinks into it. She holds her breath for a few seconds and then her small face bursts out of the surface gasping for air. She smiles, and gasps, and laughs, and asks "Did you see that, Mommy?" and there she goes again.

The madwoman sits right next to me watching her too. But I've got my eye on her.

The tub is overflowing and water runs down the tiles and onto the floor. My daughter runs her small hands on her face, pushing away wet strands of hair blocking her view. She smiles another triumphant smile and her dark eyes search for me in the small room in an air of what I understand to be well-disguised panic.

As she sits there, on the edge of the cliff, with her legs dangling as though she is a little girl on a swing, she thinks of the three of them—the madwoman, her lovely teacher, her beautiful dark-eyed daughter. She wonders how the fall would be like, with the wind in her hair and on her skin, with her crazy heart torn by the sharp rocks, with the cool water washing away the pain—her blood becoming one with her secret lover's blood.

The burst of explosions startles her. She sinks her nails into her flesh. But none of her primal instincts for survival overtakes her. She doesn't even consider running away toward safety. She abandons herself, staring at the spot where the dark skyline touches the hilltops—right where bursts of fire illuminate the darkness for brief moments each time. She lights a cigarette and focuses her look on the distant horizon, so casually as though she is watching the fireworks at the finale of a grand fiesta.

She thinks of how much she would want to touch him again—just for a brief moment. To place her palm on his cheek and maybe whisper something—anything! Maybe a stupid desire.

She thinks of her daughter lying still in the bathtub. Her features are neutral and calm as though she is dead. The madwoman leans over and stares breathless. She thinks of how much she wants to push the madwoman over the cliff. She thinks of how much she wants to sink into the water with her child—the two of them making bubbles and giggling away.

On the hill top, explosions tear open the dark sky like claws. She lights another cigarette, closes her eyes and pretends that none of these is happening. She kind of feels that if she closes her eyes long enough, she will be lost again into the night—into its alluring whispers, into the mesmerizing caresses of the summer breeze. She opens her eyes disappointed. Sirens are wailing. A fire is burning. Someone is yelling in panic;

something incomprehensible. What was a few moments ago pitch-dark and beautiful is now torched. This night is just too surreal. It can't be happening.

She picks herself up and lets her gaze travel from the small blinking lights on the top of the power station's towers to the massive fire on the hills, to the blackness of the sea beneath. She's spreading her arms as though trying to balance between the sanity she's lost and the murky waters of her messed-up mind.

She envisions herself chained-up in a dark cave. All she can see are dark shadows on its wall—a reflection. Too much time has gone by and she has forgotten. The voices and the lovely commotion of the real world reverberate against the walls of her cave and she thinks that's it! She doesn't attempt to free herself from her bonds. She is convinced that the cave, and the shadows, and the echoes *are* the world. Outside, her life walks on by casually whistling a tune, but she is unaware of it. Sometimes, for a brief moment there's a different voice inside the cave, but it is lost in the cacophony. She struggles to listen. "Did you see that, Mommy?"

She frees herself from her bonds. She runs. She runs like she's never run before.

A young man grabs her hand. He is all sweaty and naked from the waist up. He shouts something she cannot fathom. She can't make out the features of his face. The air is dense with smoke and the smell of the world burning makes her dizzy. Pieces of debris float around them glowing like fireflies.

He pulls her to the opposite direction. She follows. She has made her choice. His grip is firm and she feels safe and protected.

They push themselves with difficulty through the dried barley fields. All she can hear is their breathing as they gasp for air. All the rest is just white noise. All she can feel is his firm grip. A young, unknown boy's firm grip. She holds onto his hand as though her life depends on him and him alone. There's another blast and they fall on the ground—face down. It's cool and wet laying there idle, still holding onto each other's hand. Their coming together is marked by the trail they've left behind in the barley field.

Erato Ioannou-Moustaka is a Cypriot fiction writer with a BA in English Language and Literature from the University of Cyprus, and an MFA in Creative Writing from the University of North Carolina at Wilmington. In collaboration with the Cyprus Museum of Jacksonville North Carolina, she published Cyprus Engraved, a book on the cartography of Cyprus (2002). She has published Cats Have it All (2004) with Armida Publications, and her short stories have appeared in various literary magazines. In her work, Ioannou-Moustaka thematizes the existential problems of loneliness and alienation that plague our way of life.

Photograph by Jonathan Soch

THE DRAGON

ALINE ARONSKY

Jerry screeched to a halt and flung his bike aside. It landed with a soft thud on top of a pile of leaves.

He ran across to the nearest tree and looked back. "Let's play hide-and-seek! Onetwothree-go!" He disappeared into the dense forest.

I wasn't worried. Jerry was smart, for a six-year-old. Plus, he basically grew up in this forest. He knew it like the back of his hand.

"Coming..." I really didn't want to have to deal with him. I had homework, and my girlfriend wanted to meet up with me soon. I kicked aside a rock with my hands in my pockets. The only reason I was here is because I wanted to get Jerry away from all the screaming in the house. It isn't fair to him to have to listen to my mom and dad fight all the time.

I look around me at the familiar forest. I guess I know it like the back of my hand too. It's mid-October, the time when the colorful autumn leaves turn a sickly brown, and the chilly wind reminds you that the nice weather doesn't want to stay forever.

I don't even have to think twice to know where

Jerry went to "hide". After two minutes of walking I push aside a spiky branch to reveal a clearing, with a mammoth oak tree, and a tree house twice as old as me. Jerry has already forgotten about his game, pounding his chest, and screaming ancient jungle calls.

I sigh and find a tree to lean against. I find all his hooting and hollering kind of silly. When he gets a little older I'll make sure to tell him to wake up and realize life isn't a game.

I open my iPhone. Should've known there wouldn't be any signal here.

I look down at my big brother. He had his arms crossed, and was staring into his phone. It was stupid.

"Alec, come up and play with me! I'm Tarzan, King of the Jungle!"

He didn't answer.

Hunph. I could have fun without him.

I skipped to the other side of the tree house. There were infinite possibilities. I skimmed the tree line, looking for any enemies. Aha! A branch of leaves squirmed and twisted. It molded itself into an awful eagle, with eyes like fire and claws sharper than anything in the entire world! It spotted me and I gasped. Suddenly it stretched its wings and flew towards me. What should I do? It was coming, faster and faster! I quickly picked up a stick. But this was no ordinary stick, no, it was a sword with a shining silver blade. I looked back at the eagle. It was so close. I jumped forward and raised the blade behind my head.

"Hiya!!" Jerry's scream cut through the silence of the forest. I watched him throw a stick down to the ground where it cracked in half, the two parts flying in opposite directions.

"Victory is mine!!!" He hooted and started to climb the rope ladder down to the ground.

"Jerry, be careful. Don't fall." I winced as his foot caused one of the rungs on the ladder to break.

He ignored me, jumping down to the ground and started running circles around the tree house. His arms were spread out at his sides.

"Whoosh! Wanna help me find the treasure, Alec? You can be my noble steed!"

He screeched to a halt in front of me, panting. "Come on! First we have to defeat the dragon."

I rolled my eyes. How long would it take for him to go off on his own again?

"All right, buddy. I'll be your horse, but soon I'll be tired, then you have to go by yourself, okay?"

"Aww..." Jerry impatiently pulled at my shirt. I crouched down so he could get on my back. "Giddyup! The dragon's over there!"

"Where, where?" I laughed. I picked up a stick from the ground. "Here's a sword, you better protect yourself."

"He's over there!" Jerry gasped. "Be brave!"

I ran over to where he was pointing, then screeched to a halt when I saw a flicker of flame.

"He's there! I see him! ROARR!!" Jerry's childish voice melded into a gut-wrenching, heart-stopping snarl of a dragon. I cringed.

"Come on Alec, let's go! You can't give up now!"

I nodded. I picked up a sword of my own and charged, Jerry bouncing on my back. The dragon dodged and twisted, swung and snapped. Finally, we flung ourselves to the ground, almost out of energy. The beast was crawling towards us, smoke seeping out of its ugly nostrils.

Jerry gulped. "What should we do?"

I had an idea, and whispered into his ear. He nodded, then ran off.

The dragon stepped towards me. The forest rumbled. I was on my back, panting, the sweat falling off the tip of my nose. I wiped it off, keeping my eyes on the ugly creature.

Suddenly I saw Jerry approaching the dragon from behind. He raised his sword with both arms and flung it down with all his might, right into its emerald flank.

The monster let out a screech that sent the birds into the sky, chilling me to my very bones. With a roar he fell down on the ground. Jerry and I cut off its head together.

"That was awesome!" Jerry screamed with delight. He flung his stick away and ran off.

I wiped the sweat from my brow and turned around. When I saw the young couple in jogging clothes staring at me I started. They looked stunned, both with their eyebrows raised. The woman had her mouth wide open.

The man cleared his throat, flustered. "Aren't you a little old to be playing make-believe?" He asked.

"Me?" I asked. "I don't think you're ever too old." I pocketed my iPhone and waved goodbye to the couple, following Jerry.

I'd worry about homework later.

Aline Aronsky was born in Utah, in 1996. She grew up in Tennessee for her entire life, until two years ago, when her and her family moved to Switzerland. She is now completing her 10th Grade Year at ZIS, the Zurich International School, where she plans to graduate with a full IB Diploma. She is hoping to go to university in England, where she would like to continue as a journalist or writer.

Photograph by Sophie Fontaine

COLLECTING ART

RUPAN MALAKIN

Van Doot was a stout, groomed man, with a beard shaped like an equilateral triangle between his lower lip and chin. At noon he arrived at the artist's house, some chap named Risible, and waited until the second hand moved around to the hour on his *Patek Philippe* wristwatch before knocking with a swift and certain rap. It had taken months to find this fellow. Risible's name was always mentioned at openings and parties, exciting Van Doot's desire to see his art, which was described by a fellow collector only last week as facing fears different from others. Although Van Doot was unsure what this meant, it assuaged his belief that this artist ploughed the field of human perspicacity, or, as he liked to put it, burst from the blue waters of the mind.

After the third knock, Van Doot heard shuffled footsteps, growly coughs, and muttered expletives. The front door swung open, revealing a slight and grubby man, nervous looking, his stained white dressing gown hanging open to the waist, the end of an extinguished cigarette bent between nicotine-stained fingers.

"Are you the artist?" asked the collector.

"Well I'm not the fucking vicar," Risible replied, before coughing into his fist and wiping the mucus down the front of his gown.

After a moment's silence, Van Doot asked if he may come in. When Risible turned and shrugged, the collector shuddered at the dandruff in his hair, the flaking skin on the red nape of his neck.

They passed through a hallway stinking of turpentine and urine into a lounge that, if the collector were kind, may be described as humble. A beige sofa hunkered in the corner, threadbare and torn, the wood bursting through the fabric as though the frame were trying to make an escape. The artist waved towards it. "You wanna sit?" he said.

"No, I'm fine," replied the collector.

"You wanna drink?"

"No, I'm fine."

"Well, what do you want?"

Van Doot stroked the point of his beard with a white-gloved hand. "I was hoping, perhaps, to see..."

Risible sneered. "So, you want to see, do you? And to buy?"

Not wanting to play his hand too early – the collector had bargained all over the world – he replied that maybe he would if the artist had something worthy to sell.

"As you wish," said the artist, and shambled from the room.

He returned with a stack of canvases and dropped them on the floor by the collector's feet. When Risible squatted beside them, Van Doot, reluctantly, joined.

"This," Risible said, showing the first canvas, "Is Dog Chewing A Bull's Penis."

It was a decent representation, done in the realist style, similar to Rembrandt, of a dog, a German Shepherd maybe, chewing. Of the penis, however, there was nothing. Van Doot mused over this, and then said, "How do you know what the dog is chewing?"

The artist looked disgusted. "I have told you what it is chewing. Is that not enough?"

"Of course, of course," said Van Doot. He put it to one side and examined the next canvas, this one depicting something blue, and apparently bulging. "And what do you call this piece?"

"I call it, Old Woman Wearing Blue Lycra."

Van Doot stared at the painting. "But where is the old woman?"

"Do you not see? The old woman is in your mind!"

"But what about the painting?"

"That, perhaps, is her thigh."

"Fascinating," said the collector.

Van Doot studied every canvas – a hairless armpit called The Clean-Shaved Doctor, an empty bowl called Still Life With Apples And Lemons, Eaten – and many others. His joints aching, Van Doot stood and staggered backwards, slumping onto the worn sofa. It was true. This work was different, original. Magnificent.

Before he could stop himself, he made a generous offer for the entire collection.

Risible told him to double it.

The collector cried, "I'll take them!"

On the morning of the exhibition, Van Doot left detailed instructions with Alain, his assistant, on how he wanted the paintings arranged. All day, the collector fizzed with excitement, enrapt by visions of how the paintings would be received by his peers, so much so that his barber admonished him for ginning while he shaped the point of Van Doot's tiny triangular beard.

When evening came, the gallery's reception began to fill. Over champagne and canapés Van Doot mingled with the art world's finest. Soon the moment arrived. The collector opened the doors and led his guests through.

Van Doot gazed around the room in shock.

Dog Chewing A Bull's Penis was hung beside the title This Is Not A Painting. The Clean-Shaved Doctor was now called Old Woman Wearing Lycra.

Mortified, the collector hurried around the room.

They were all wrong!

He covered his face with his hands, holding back tears, unable to believe his reputation, cultivated over thirty years, was to be destroyed in an instant. He waited for the mocking laughter to start.

The art collector slowly lowered his hands. To his surprise, he saw his guests gazing at the paintings, emitting the comforting umms and ahhs of artistic appreciation. One of his fellow collectors took his arm and led him to Still Life With Apples And Lemons, Eaten – now a painting of a steak dinner that should have been called The Night Before A Good Shit – and said, "Wherever did you find this chap, Quentin. Such meaning! Such endeavour! He really does back flip around the borders of the soul. Quite remarkable…"

"Indeed," said Van Doot, smiling now. "He is a quite remarkable chap."

Rupan is a short writer of tall stories. Say hello at www.rupanmalakin.com, or @rupanmalakin.

Photograph by George Erws

A NIGHT WITH HUGH AND KEATS

JULIE NOBLE

In the low forgiving light, Hugh's stretching hand is illuminated by the entire focus of my attention, until it seems as bright as the white, gloved hands of a stage magician. One of those who dresses in black, and performs the sleight of hand in front of a dark screen, all the better to practise his deception upon the brain's perception.

While I watch, anticipation keeps me silent, but I cannot prevent my body from showing signs of impatience: my jaws condense with tension, while my tongue slips quickly under the groove of my top lip.

Hugh's confident fingers curve around the glass bottle, secure as the grasp of an anxious mother. A deft twist of the wrist, arcing the vessel through a rainbow, brings the open mouth of the bottle in front of my eyes so that I can see the opulent fluid swirling invitingly.

"Smell," he orders brusquely, "and try to maintain your focus. The brain has to be *fully* engaged to sense the finer qualities of the wine."

At last I am able to take hold of the precious object, cradling it with the reverence due to a communion chalice. I breathe in deeply to catch the intoxicating scent and instantly my brain flares into glorious life, as furiously as flames firing a furnace. I recognise the approach of satisfaction, however short-lived.

"This is perfect," I declare quickly, "I'll give it ten out of ten."

Eagerness forces me to be generous, though tonight I am particularly delighted with the sensations given by this vintage's scented bouquet. The invisible molecules which I have imbibed are so richly evocative of those lost days of summer sunshine that they even revive a few lines from the poem I once knew word for word:

"*O, for a draught of vintage! Tasting of Flora and the country green, Dance… song and sunburnt mirth…*"

When we were studying Keats for exams, I was like the nightingale he speaks to, blissfully ignorant of "*the weariness, the fever and the fret*".

Then my mind was trained to be as ordered as an architect's plan, but now I believe that sometimes it is better not to know where you will wake or sleep.

"*A beaker full of the warm south… That I might drink, and leave the world unseen.*"

With the remedy right under my nose, I begin lifting the prized liquid to my lips, but my companion is vigorously shaking his head.

"No, no, no! That is *not* how you do it."

When I don't immediately return the bottle, Hugh becomes agitated. His hands flap so pathetically that I am forced to stop. There's a minute of indecision but a reminiscence of long ago lessons in etiquette exerts its effect, and my hand wavers.

Hugh shudders with relief, shaking his head once more, and jerking a hand towards me as though I am one of those irritating insects we are plagued with. Instead of being angered, I find myself impressed that he is still a perfectionist, despite all.

"You must do this much more slowly; give the vapour sufficient time to lift the aroma. Let me show you!"

Again Hugh waves his wrist impatiently, and now the movement has become so exaggerated that I have to stifle the urge to chuckle. I am fidgety in the way children struggle to contain themselves under authority. The fierceness of his bristling eyebrows is comical. As a child I would have laughed, as a younger man I would have mocked, but I have learned a great deal in recent years. Suffering can bring about one of two outcomes, that of compassion or that of bitterness. I prefer to hope that I have distilled the former.

Gradually I manage to lower my hand and force my arm muscles to extend in his direction, though my teeth are grinding in frustration. Hugh quickly relieves me of the vessel, and I watch my newly empty fingers linger in the place where it was, trembling still and wafting hopefully, like a waiting sea anemone.

At least The Expert does not disappoint.

Hugh begins his performance by giving a sumptuous authoritative sigh, closing his eyes decisively and breathing out as if his life is draining out of him. He pauses for a moment to savour the death-like state. I can understand that; I'm often more than "*half in love with easeful death*" myself. Finally, with still closed eyes, he lifts his nose over the wine and begins systematic in-breathing, leisurely yet measured, like a sun-dried Mediterranean fisherman standing alone in his low boat, hauling a line,

"Delicate aroma," he murmurs from his reverie. Jealously I notice every alteration in his face: the smoothing of the forehead, the flaring of the nostrils, even detecting the movement of the eye behind the lids, twitching the surface skin like fish tails flickering under water.

"Floral overtones." Sniff, sniff, s-t-r-e-t-c-h-e-d s-n-i-f-f.

"And something else..." His head tilts quizzically while he swirls the liquid, casting for the elusive odour hidden under the surface,

"Citrus!" He announces, finally opening his eyes and looking at me for approval. I smile, and Hugh nods eagerly as he reels out his opinion, cheerfully confident in his assertion,

"The classic combination of a Riesling raised in a cold climate. Good, or should I be saying *Gut*?"

Hugh grins triumphantly at this little display of his long disused language ability and raises a hand tremulous with anticipation. He absorbs the liquid slowly, in tiny but continuous proportions, like a storm drain devoting itself to a trickle. Anxious for my opportunity, I shift my buttocks.

"Ah! What delights! The nose does not disappoint the palate! The aroma continues, and becomes… peaches!"

"Sounds wonderful," I say curtly, with a crisp hint of impatience that is lost on him. Hugh grasps the bottle ever tighter and lifts again. Drinking properly this time, I note, not sipping.

"Isn't scent the most evocative of memory prompters?" he muses suddenly, "So intriguing how the mere inhalation of a wine's bouquet can give one the most delightful visions of a distant era?" He flourishes the bottle in my direction and I am hopeful, but all I receive are his thoughts, and these he bestows liberally. Hugh can wax as lyrically and lavishly as any one of those legendary literary bohemians who spent their day lounging and drinking in the name of creativity.

I fight the desire to get up, grab the bottle, and walk away. While I rail inwardly, he continues, brimming with reminiscence.

"They had this at my son's wedding," he says proudly, "I helped them choose the wine list. It was a wonderful day…"

Like confetti falling about my ears he describes the perfection of the church setting, the freshness of the flowers his wife had arranged, his beautiful daughters as the bridesmaids.

"I cannot see what flowers are at my feet, Nor what soft incense hangs upon the boughs."

It is a luxurious concoction he serves, idyllic, and so wonderfully presented that for a moment, - a brief moment, as swift as a bird, disturbed, flying off into a forest - I think I can smell the sweet, sickening scent of the lilies falling onto the tables.

"But here there is no light."

As he begins to venture into philosophy, his thin snippets of wisdom, no matter how valuable their pertinence or perception, fall unrecorded and unremembered. These days, neither the "*viewless wings of poesy*", nor the mightiest heart-felt sentiments, delicately described, are sufficient to release my dull brain; only one thing will suffice. Now, despite my efforts at attention, I can barely hear him. My entire concentration is focused on one thing only, and I'm not letting it out of sight. In a matter of minutes my patience is rewarded, his hand slackens, the bottle tips, and I see a chance. Bending forward, my empty palm slides under his fingers and the bottle is mine.

He's still talking. Murmuring about missing out, or passing out, but I don't care, I'm not listening. Instead my entire perception is concentrated on enjoying the sanctified seconds of anticipation.

I remember what they said when I had the breakdown:

'Find the positives'

'Learn to live in the moment'

Good advice, especially for where I am now.

At least when biblical Ruth stood, "*sick for home*", amidst the soothing, waving beauty of a golden corn field, her future was all around her in that bountiful harvest. Here, in the dark, dust-bin gloom of a back street, long after hours, there is no friendly bustle, nor opportunity. No kindly restaurant owner around to scatter the gift of food. If found, we are shoo-ed and shouted away, as though we are dogs. The voices grate, the arms wave angrily, but they never actually touch us. Even the rats resent us.

But as I said, I've learnt to find the positives in the moment, and just as well. Looking forward is as futile as expecting the barred, dark exit we are sitting beside to suddenly spring open, exhibiting welcoming arms and a banquet spread upon white linen.

I know that's what is inside because in my former days, I used to enter the front entrance of this very restaurant. The Maître D' was as close as a friend, welcoming me into the sumptuous surroundings. The waiters all smiled when they saw me.

But what is the point in recalling it all? The stiff, starched whiteness of the tablecloths, the cosiness of the jewelled candlelight, or the brilliance of those "*beaded bubbles winking at the brim.*"

It's a pity I forgot that bubbles are only filled with emptiness too.

"Where but to think is to be full of sorrow."

All the doors are closed now. Every last one. It was the purple-stained mouth that got me into trouble, the mouth that kept talking long after any wisdom had gone.

What I have left is the wine.

I force my mind to remember Hugh's lesson, telling myself I am not yet sunk so low that I can't appreciate it. Trying to emulate my tutor, I incline my face and raise the bottle to meet me. I greet the top of the longed-for vessel by pausing at air-kissing distance, nosing politely into the neck, breathing as slowly as I dare.

At last I can truly smell the floral bouquet. Only now can I imbibe. As the cold rim of glass meets my chilled lips, the fragrance fuses with the odours of our surroundings: the buckets full of silver service surplus, the sweet aroma of sugared sauces mingling with the tangy salad dressings, the bags splitting with the weight of used cleaning rags, an acidic whiff with a hint of lemon.

We have emptied the crates containing the bottles for tonight, but we will be back tomorrow. We don't care if they are half-full, or half-empty, just as long as they are there.

Hugh was right about the taste. As I swallow, I swear I can feel the round softness of peaches furry on the palate. The rich liquid certainly fills with as much satisfaction as any meal I ever ate here. The grape variety swirls down my throat, refreshing as a waterfall. My stomach gurgles and grunts, muttering in shocked acknowledgement, like my father at a pleasant surprise.

Within moments the alcohol floods my bloodstream, soothing and cushioning. I close my eyes, savouring the thickening warmth of my senses, the familiar comfort of the drowsy numbness. Suddenly I am ageless and painless, flowing with well-being.

"Now more than ever it seems rich to die,

To cease upon the midnight with no pain."

As consciousness departs, my last thoughts are with Keats.

"That I might drink, and leave the world unseen,

Fade far away, dissolve, and quite forget."

Primarily, I'm a wife and mother. With five children between the ages of three and twenty-one, a hard-working husband and a family business, home life is busy and productive. Before children, I studied Psychology at Lancaster University. After a variety of jobs, I now write while the youngest two are at school. I have had work published in magazines and won the 2010 She Magazine Short Story Competition. Before that, I self-published Talli's Secret, about dyspraxia, the Brontës and bereavement, which was Whitbread long-listed: website www.tallissecret.com. I believe the best things in life are family, friends and following your dream!

Photograph by Jorge Losada

UNDER THE SKYSIGNS

Gerard Urquhart

It wasn't the dead tom-cat. It wasn't that. Lying in the gutter, fur matted by the moisture from the haar that curled itself about the empty street. Its head bent at an unnatural angle over the drain cover, eyes half closed as if squinting through the grille for a glimpse of potential prey down below. It wasn't the plastic bag that half-covered its broken body like a cheap funeral shroud. The thought almost made him force a smile. But he didn't. The black-backed gull across the street, stationary, stoic, eyed him with suspicion - the mourner that only turns out for the free sandwiches and drams after. It remained silent. He was thankful for that. He continued to wander, wondering whether the dustman would notice the animal before it became trapped in the brush turbines that swept the gutter. He hoped so. There was no indication of whether it had bounced or not.

He awoke again as glass crunched underfoot. And noted, as he always did, that shattered glass from a car window always appears emerald green against a grey wash of concrete. The coloured twist of cord dangling from the central console

- the severed umbilical. The rock in the passenger seat, waiting patiently to be taken to the station. No comment, officer. It wasn't that. Or the memory of the comfort he'd felt as a child when he found a piece of an old, green beer bottle on the sands, worn smooth by the tides, no longer able to cut and jar. Placing it carefully in his pocket. Him being called a tinker by his older sister when he returned home, laden with feathers, shells, glass and sand-planed oak. Hiding them out of embarrassment. Returning to them to find them gone. No, it wasn't that.

Moving again as the low sun stole glances at the street through the slow-clearing fog. It's gaping, mocking fire-toothed maw blinding him momentarily before retreating again behind its thin veil. A faint suggestion of iridescence, vainly reflected in a dirty shop window that no longer held any store, shimmered across the curled, yellowing poster for a travelling circus. The cartoon ringmaster's once sprightly moustache now rippled and sagging around the edges of the mouth. It wasn't that. He didn't have the energy to catch his own reflection. In the weight of the half-light he didn't see the sunken cheeks, the eyes that were too big for the skull, the atrophied frame. From the doorway, the sharp reek of urine hung fresh in the cool air. He coughed. Once was enough. The now-familiar tang of iron upon his tongue. He'd had enough of coughing. Left. Right.

The hot choke of a burning cigarette was just

beginning to find its mark when the van hit him. He saw it coming. His feet had chosen that moment to relegate responsibility and were found waiting on a directive. None came. Just time for the fleeting observation: 'Aye, that wasn't a great place to cross. Blind corner.' And in that moment he had it, had it whole; the whys and wherefores; the muttering retreats. Replays on loop, the fastidious editor at work; the revisionist historian lecturing to empty rows; the forgotten batteries from clocks, incontinent in their dotage, pooling fissured secrets upon the mantelpiece amongst empty frames - light momently illuminating them from between the cracks in warped shutters; hours spent turning the hands and turning them still, in time with a drum that was never comfortable in its own skin. Indeed, there will be time. Too little. Too much. Aligned in each instant he wished to repeat.

As the tail lights receded into the distance, his final thought was of the cat. He hoped the dustman would notice him there.

Gerard Urquhart spends much of his time thinking himself elsewhere, lapses into solipsism far too often and wouldn't be all that fussed if an apocalypse razed the foundations and we had to start all over again.

Photograph by Michel Nguie

THE GUARDIAN

Gareth Barsby

I would like to call myself a man of simple tastes. Though I may incessantly indulge in the pleasures of television and the internet, I have been known to say that the best things in life are free, the wonders of nature are often overlooked and all that. You'd be surprised how many people still react to cliché; I told a friend all that and she looked at me like I was one of those deep, poetic souls so many people like to pretend to be. And yes, I suppose I'm one of those pretenders too. When I go outside and admire a flower field, I get a tiny little pang of superiority.

But I don't take photographs just to show I'm better than all those people who incessantly watch TV and munch down Doritos. I'm not really sure why I do it really. I liked doing it when I was a kid – Action Man in stupid poses captured for posterity – but I didn't know why I did it then, either. When you're a kid and you like doing something, you don't ask why, you just do it. I've taken this philosophy to my old age, and now my computer is loaded with countless pictures of flowers, old buildings and roads just because they were there and I had a camera.

So one Saturday, with no work to do, the scenery not moving an inch from where it was and me still having a camera, I decided I would take some more pictures. I had emptied my picture card last month, and it had been silently begging me to fill it up again, so out I went. It was on the first step out of my house that I took my first picture: the light on my porch. Just in case I don't find anything else worthy, I guess.

Then I went and asked myself what I was going to do with the photographs I was going to take. The first answer I gave myself was that I was going to look at them when I was on my computer and had nothing better to do. Then the cynical little man that lives in my brain responded by saying that I rarely ever do that anyway. But there surely is something I can do with what I take, isn't there? I could put them on some stock photo website to see how many people would actually use it. Aren't there forums for this type of thing?

So anyway, I walked out of my home towards somewhere I had been rarely, but had gotten some pretty nifty photos from. Like that old neighbourhood that isn't too far – loads of decaying buildings with their windows and doors boarded up, some good old urban rot. I did actually walk in that direction, but then I remembered that I saw that place as more a 'night' place. The best pictures from there were taken at night as it made it look like the buildings were haunted. What fun I had shining a torch on them at various angles.

Instead of going there, I let my body choose for me. Crossing the road without even looking, I found myself heading in the direction of that wheat field outside of town. It was quite a walk, but that place did hold a certain sense of nostalgia for me, as I did take walks beside it on hot summer's days. Although the journey there did make my legs hurt, I went along. I even took a few pictures along the way of things that caught my interest – a store mannequin wearing a stupid ensemble, an ice cream shop I remember eating at – but soon I had reached my destination.

While the sky may have been cluttered with grey clouds, the smooth bobbing of the wheat and their golden colour reminded me of the idyllic summers so often portrayed in greeting cards and paintings. It looked like Oz, where Dorothy found the Scarecrow. Just ripe for the camera-clicking. Though I knew I probably shouldn't, I stepped into the field, disturbing some neatly erect stalks as I barged through. Click went my camera as I caught a picture of the golden soldiers. Click went my camera as I contrasted their bright colour with the dismal sky. The important piece of a summertime past, preserved on a card.

Then I noticed the doll.

A large doll, standing among the wheat like I was. One of those life-sized plastic dolls with the stare and the light glistening on its synthetic skin. It looked like a fairy. Someone must have thrown it out, I thought, or decided it would be funny if it was propped up there. Maybe it was put there to deter people like me.

Nonetheless, my finger twitched at the button, moving as if it was about to stroke a parrot's head. I knew a photo op when I saw one; if I posted this on a forum, people would talk about how it represents lost innocence or something of that nature. I could even fiddle around with it on Paint.Net, give it a monochrome hue to make it look really solemn. And people say photography is simple.

I take a picture of the doll, and my eyes focus on my camera's screen.

It moved closer.

Turning my eyes away from the camera, I saw the doll inches away from me. Seeing it so close made me drop my camera and twist my body to the other direction. As I held my hands against my face, I chortled hoarsely, as if that would dispel the vision, but I heard deep breathing behind me, and something slide against my thigh.

A human finger.

I chortled again, telling myself that this was just some stupid kid playing a joke – a thought which did cause a prick of embarrassment within my gut – so I opened my eyes and turned to pick up my camera. The doll – the kid –had moved slightly closer, and while it was wearing a mask of a doll's head, its hands were indeed flesh.

"Okay, kid, look..."

The child lifted its arm, shaking like a mechanical toy, its head jolting backwards and back up again. It pointed an accusing finger at me, and then stood perfectly still like the doll it resembled. It didn't shake, it didn't even seem to be breathing. It just stood there frozen, pointing that finger in my direction, its lack of movement emphasised by the rustling of the nearby trees.

I ran.

Well, I didn't sprint all the way back home, I ran from that field and upon reaching town, stopped to catch my breath and ponder on what I had seen. I checked my camera again, and there it was, the kid with the doll mask almost filling up the whole screen. Faced with the frozen smile again, I promptly deleted the photo off of my camera, is if that would destroy the being once and for all. A wonderful thing, technology.

So I returned home to recover after that strange little incident, putting my camera aside for the rest of the day. While the doll-headed thing and its movement had left me with a shaking stomach and a warping brain, I still told myself to return to the field that night. It did still hold some fond memories for me, and I didn't want it to become permanently attached to some kid playing a trick.

With the streets bathed in darkness and the image of a doll mask with an eerie smile beginning it, this outing felt more like an adventure than the one earlier today. Feeling like I was setting off on an exciting journey did distil the chills I received from the rendezvous earlier today until they vanished altogether, and soon I had tricked myself into thinking I was just going outside for the hell of it. In fact, I even regretted not bringing my camera. I love the way the road looks under the streetlights.

Then I saw the fire.

I had reached the wheat field and it was on fire. Or rather, a large bonfire now sat in the middle of the field, highlighting the figures gathered around it. The doll kid, and four more doll kids. Each of them looked exactly like the other; same clothes, same build, same mask.

They all looked at me.

Gareth Barsby is a graduate of the University of Chester who enjoys writing stories and reading them aloud. He currently does volunteer work for a Birmingham magazine and writes film and television reviews.

Photograph by Nicole O'Connor

LILAC AND MAXI

Pablo Fuentes

The pale lilac on this picture could not match the feeling of loss it brought to me. I used to think the place on the picture meant nothing to anyone but myself. I used to believe our relationship had been secret and remained secret all the way to its tragic end.

He would sneak through those windows on hot summer nights, and that we would run quietly to the park where we would pick one of the more isolated benches.

Those nights were not pale lilac as this picture, but varying shades of blue and gray. Sitting on the bench, we would be looking at the stars while holding hands, and this simple act brought peace and happiness to my life, also filling it with passion, hope and a few times heartfelt laughter.

What those nights meant for him I will never know. He was always very reserved and quiet and would seldom talk about his feelings, his family or anything else. He would just sit there with me and hold hands, even when they got sweaty and sticky, he would not let go before I did.

The day he killed himself I remember running

to his house and looking at the windows with quiet desperation. I was half expecting him to peak out and tell me that he had staged his death so that we could run away together. But the windows were dark and I just stood there feeling foolish. He had never promised anything, so why did I feel so betrayed?

A few weeks passed and his wife (widow by then, I guess) put bars on the windows, and then a few weeks after that she put an air conditioning unit. Finally, the other window was boarded from the inside. I gave more meaning to her actions than what they had, I am sure.

Do not ask me who wrote his name on the window. All I can tell you is that it wasn't me. I suspect it was probably the same person who sent me this picture through the mail today.

With what purpose was it sent to me? Camaraderie? A brutal confession that it wasn't just me who had his love? A clumsy attempt to mourn together?

Well... I don't want to find out. For now I find some peace just by looking at the beautiful picture and remembering me standing there waiting for him to come out on hot summer nights. I find comfort in knowing that even though it was always very dark, the wall and its windows looked bright and blue to me, so different from the pale lilac on this picture.

Pablo Fuentes is 35 years old and works as a Chemical Engineer. He graduated from the US in 1998 and has lived in eight countries since. He works for an insurance company and writes short stories in his free time. Pablo Fuentes is now living in Madrid, Spain.

Photograph by Manuela Trevia

STONE DIVIDE

ANDREA WEINER

I smell like the inside of a new car; the leather is smooth and weighs heavy on my shoulders. I try breathing through my mouth to avoid the nauseating scent. But then he yells at me to snap my mouth shut, he says I look like a hungry dog. I roll my eyes and bring my jaw together.

The faux fur makes my neck itchy, and I want to scratch so badly. I angle my head forward and slightly down to avoid the itch. It works and he loves it. The wind starts to blow gently and the fur tickles now. I ignore his praise and lift a hand to pat down the fur. He furrows his brow and I drop my hand quickly.

The silver in my ears is foreign and heavy. I haven't worn earrings this large and cumbersome in so long. I swear I can feel the skin in my ears stretching. I wonder if when we're done I'll have gaping holes in my ears from them. I wonder when we'll even be done.

He tells me to make love to the wall. He tells me to make him want me. He tells me to be sexy. I don't know how to do any of those things. I feel awkward as I lean against the rough rocks with a sappy look on my face. He scowls again and tells me I'm doing it wrong. He says to pout and have desire in my eyes. I drape myself over the wall and try to do what he wants.

More clicks go off, and the flash blinds me again and again. I'm losing my balance and I stumble trying to regain stable footing. He curses and yells; all I can do is focus on his flaring nostrils. They entertain me, and I don't even hear the words he spits out, but I watch those big nostrils open and close over and over.

The words die down and the camera is back at his eye. I wonder where the passage behind me leads. I wonder if there are people at the end of it curious as to who is standing in their doorway. I wonder if I could walk through it and find something amazing. Perhaps there are piles of gold and money and no one knows because it's do desolate looking that no one dare venture down that way. I turn my head to look into the darkness and am brought back by his angry yells again.

All the water pills he stuffs down my throat have taken effect. I need to pee now. I swear we've been at this for nearly three hours and no break. I focus my gaze on him as he kneels down to change the film over. I have a desperate desire to run away, through the archway. I want to get away from this; this Hell that I exist in.

He calls me over to him and I gladly walk away from the stone. He says we're done for the day, but we have another job that night. He says I can't eat until the job is over. Water can be drunk, if and only if I take more of those pills. I agree and he stands up, grasps my shoulders tightly and looks me in the eyes. He tells me he'll know if I eat, so I better be on my best behavior. I nod and he embraces me.

His hand cups the back of my head and pulls me into his chest. This is the worst part. I know this routine better than anything he wants me to do. His hand slinks around to my face and he tilts my head upward. His eyes are dark, and I can see my reflection in them. I will myself not to tremble, it only angers him more. And then it is happening, his rough stubble grating against my porcelain skin. His lips pressed against mine, and his tongue enters my mouth. He tastes like stale cigarettes and remnants of beer drunk hours ago. His other hand snakes around my waist as I let myself get used. I become a rag doll, all my limbs are loose and I contort to his will. I hate myself.

He finishes exploiting me and pushes me away from him. The taste in my mouth is bitter and I feel sick. I briskly walk towards the trailer and let myself in to relieve myself. The little corner bathroom is small and nearly impossible to enter. I walk in and close the little door behind me. I turn around and lower myself onto the toilet.

I finish and look into the mirror. My skin is pink where his face rubbed against mine. I feel so dirty; I wash my hands and scrub the soap into my skin. Grasping the corners of the sink I study my face. I had beautiful lively brown eyes, they're quite dull now. My hair is some ridiculous shade of red; I can barely remember what color it is naturally. My eyebrows are thin and even, not a single stray hair is there. My collar bones stick out prominently and I hate them. I hate the hollow dips that are created around them. I bare my teeth. They would make any dentist proud; pure white and aligned evenly. My nose was small and appropriate for the build of my face. I was text book beautiful.

A knock on the door snapped me out of self-criticism. He yelled at me to come out, and accused me of eating. I opened the door and hurried out. I rushed past him and out of the trailer. I was walking and then jogging and finally I broke into a sprint. I could feel my high heels wiggling beneath me and I kicked them off running as hard as I could back to the stone wall. I was going to find out what was through that passageway. I was going to escape. I was going to be free. I was going to find myself again. I was going to be happy.

Andrea Weiner is 21 years old and was born and raised in Connecticut, where she still resides. She has been writing since she could spell, and she has always had a taste for fiction. She works hard at two jobs and is a part-time nursing student at her local community college. She takes pride in what she does, whether it's work-related or creative release. She has always enjoyed reading others' work and writing her own pieces.

Photograph by Dario Zanetti

GHOSTS

Sam Graham

Glenn couldn't tell if the guy lying faced-down on the curbside, bathed orange by the streetlights, was alive or dead. One of his legs was moving, but that could have just been a nervous twitch. His head was slumped between the curb and the graffiti and rust-covered skip, and dirty water pooled inches from his feet at the edge of the tarmac. The tatty duffel coat he was wearing made Glenn think he was a tramp, but the fairly clean trainers on his feet said otherwise. Maybe he was just poor. That was the conclusion he stuck with. Glenn had never seen a real dead person before, and the thought that he might be standing just a few paces from one now terrified him.

He looked around. There was nobody else on this little side-street except for him and this guy and aside from the muffled bass thumping from the nightclubs a few streets over, it was silent. The air was cold and the night sky was cloudless; it seemed to make it colder somehow. Glenn wanted to check the man's pulse, or at least call him an ambulance, but he didn't do either. Instead he told himself it wasn't his business, and ran. By the end of that night, he'd wish to God he'd have just called an ambulance when he had the chance.

As Glenn reached the top end of the street where it joined the main road, he looked back. The guy was still lying down in the gutter, unmoving. Glenn leaned against a post-box while he reconsidered calling 999. He knew he should, it was the least he could do, and besides, he'd want someone to do the same for him. His heart was beating fast, almost palpitating and underneath his clothes he was hot and clammy. He looked down. In his hand was a twenty pound note. A fairly new one too, it seemed, no creases, no little tears in the edges. Crisp.

I've got to, he told himself.

As he took his mobile out to call an ambulance, the unmistakably bright Battenberg colours of a police car turned a corner, onto the main road. Glenn dialled, put the phone to his ear, then looked down the street at the body, then at the car, back at the body, the car, the body, the ringing in his ear. The phone picked up and Glenn cancelled it, dropped it back in his pocket.

He stuffed the twenty note in with his phone and headed home as quick as he could, reminding himself that that guy down there was none of his business, that he shouldn't get involved. He had his own problems to sort out before he could move on to anyone else's.

When Glenn got home, took his coat off, threw his wallet on the settee and sat down. He realised he hadn't opened the post that came that morning. It was right next to him. He looked down at it, particularly at the green rhombuses that lined the edge of the envelopes, signifying them as being from the council. They were the reason he hadn't opened them, the reason he didn't want to, and the reason he wouldn't. Those green markings were the government's sneer at him, the sharp teeth just on the inside of the biscuit tin. He knew what the letters inside would be like: Dear Mr Bennings, then words like 'final', followed by you owe these this, them that, all ending arbitrary dates that all meant they were screwing him.

Glenn sighed, then picked up the letters and dropped them in the top drawer of the cabinet along with the other important post. Once they were out of sight, he went into the kitchen and opened the bottle of whiskey he'd got for Christmas, then poured some into a mug with decorated with autumn leaves. He didn't mix it with anything. He took it back to the settee, lit a Lambert and relaxed into the cushions. The combination of whiskey and smoke ravaged his throat as he took it in turns to finish them both off.

Was the man dead? He asked himself. The image of that guy in the gutter hadn't left his mind. Was he actually dead? If he was, it doesn't matter. There's nothing a paramedic could've done; he'll still be dead in the morning when somebody finds him. What if he was alive though? He might have lived if I'd have called an ambulance. At least had a better chance, anyway…

Glenn hated to admit it to himself; the thought even disgusted him a little, but he'd have preferred it if the guy was dead. It made his conscience that bit easier to deal with.

Before he went to bed, he made a point to chew on two rennies and take some paracetamol to take the edge off the burning in his throat.

It was almost two in the morning when Glenn got into bed and closed his eyes. By half four he was still tossing and turning. He couldn't tell what was keeping him awake more, the guilt or the fear, both about the guy in the gutter. The image in his head seemed more real now than when he had lived it. Now his brain had had the time to process the image and make out every nuance from those few scant seconds he was there, he saw more things like the scuff marks on the sides of his trainers that at the time he thought looked so new, the chewing gum stuck to the pavement, blackened by years of weather and being trodden on, the spray paint on the side of the skip that read 'WOODTWOK'. Forcing himself to try and forget only made it more prominent and soon it made his temples throb, despite the painkillers he'd taken.

One thing he couldn't discern though, even with the vividness of the image in his head, was whether the guy was alive or dead.

At five am Glenn got up, started to pour himself another cup of whiskey, then decided to take the whole bottle into the living room instead. He lit up a smoke and put it away in less than a minute. He lit another straight after, the fingers that held it trembling, and leaned back into the settee again, and closed his eyes.

Who was he? Glenn asked himself. He found himself answering.

He was probably called something like Samuel Patrice, probably. Probably a French dad and an English mam or something. She'd have been from here and they'd have met when he came over for business or something. He was probably twenty-three, birthday in the winter, a few weeks ago maybe.

"Nope, birthday's in September." The Samuel that Glenn was picturing in his head said. Glenn tipped the whiskey bottle upside down and downed more of it than he really should have in one gulp.

"What do you do?" Glenn asked him.

"Dropped out of university five months ago, trying to start my own business."

Glenn was surprised to hear that the Samuel in his head had a thick Geordie accent. University explains what he's doing around here, he thought.

"What'd you do at uni?" Glenn lit a third cig.

"Environmental Management."

"What's that?"

"No idea, that's why I left. Figured earnin's better than learnin', as they say."

Glenn nodded.

Samuel continued. "Was gonna start a business importing American shoes and flogging them off cheap here. Get a little place with tiny overheads."

"Why shoes?"

"Why not? Everybody wears 'em. Nation-wide market, in a way."

Glenn couldn't find a point to argue against. He drank some more and slouched back further into the cushions. In his head he imagined Samuel sitting in the armchair opposite him. It half-faced the television and half-faced him and the settee. Samuel sat sideways in it, with one knee up on the bottom cushion, so that he could look at him squarely.

"What were you doing down that little street tonight, Sam?"

"Samuel, actually. I was at a mate's house. It got a bit late and I'd gone and left my wallet at home, so couldn't get a taxi. Decided to walk home; it's not far."

"You get jumped on your way home or something?"

Samuel said nothing. He didn't have to.

Glenn cleared his throat to get rid of the uncomfortable silence. The whiskey bottle was down to one third. He took another large gulp. "So, what you do at your mate's?"

"Watched *Heat*. Good film; one of my favourites I'd say."

"Never seen it. Heard of it though. Mine's *Italian Job*. All time classic."

Samuel nodded. The silence came back and Glenn found himself struggling for things to say. "So… What other stuff you like?"

"Why? OK, roast chicken with gravy, 'Country House' by Blur, black coffee."

"Ah right." Glenn ran his tongue around the inside of his mouth. He was too numbed and intoxicated by the whiskey to feel how much drinking it burned. He had some more after he dabbed the cig out in the tin ashtray on the settee and lit a fourth.

"What about you?" Samuel said, looking at him, staring at him. Glenn couldn't bring himself to meet his gaze.

"Are you alive, Samuel?" Glenn said. Samuel's eyes twitched, shocked by the abruptness of the question. He paused for what Glenn thought was a long time. Glenn was on the edge of his seat, waiting for the answer. He couldn't take the waiting; he needed to know now.

"What do you think?" Was all that Samuel said.

"I'm sorry." Glenn dropped his head in his hands. The cold glass of the whiskey bottle pressed against his temple. "I'm so sorry."

"What for?" Samuel didn't say it as a question; he sounded more like he was forcing a confession.

"I've done everything they asked, Sam. I just

couldn't play their game anymore. You've got to understand."

"What do you mean?"

"I never thought, in the whole world, things'd end up like this." Glenn felt the tears backing up and his lip start to quiver. He tried to stop himself, but it was too late. He was over the line now. "I needed the money. You had that twenty on you, didn't you?"

"Yeah. It wasn't mine, hence not getting a taxi home."

"I've done everything the government's been asking me to do. I filled in their forms, I went to that bloody building every fortnight, but I've never got anything back. It would have been nice to know they're not bothered. At least it'd have stopped me guessing. For months now with nothing. Nothing here, nothing there, but they still keep hassling me, and they know I can't pay them. I tell them all the time, I haven't got it. Then there're the others: gas, electricity, everyone who can milk me dry is trying to. All because someone dropped the ball and lost some stupid little piece of paper, now it's all my fault and my mess to clean up. I can't get another one. I've tried, but they won't believe me." Glenn looked up at Samuel. He couldn't make him out from the tears blurring his eyes, but he could tell he didn't look at all sympathetic.

"And you're not even fucking real. You're out there, on that street, dead."

"Say it." Samuel, in his head, said.

"I know you're dead, Sam."

"Say it."

"Because I did it." After the words had left his mouth, the realisation made his insides go cold and numb. He leaned forward on the edge of the settee, cradled his head in his hands and wept. He had no idea how long he was in that state for. It didn't matter anyway; it was all out in the open now.

When he recollected himself he looked around the small living room, at the empty chair that half-faced him and the television, at the cabinet where he'd stuffed the important letters, at the almost empty whiskey bottle, and he realised he was shivering. He took a deep breath and poured the whiskey down his throat, drinking nearly all that was left in one go.

It had all happened so fast, he hadn't had the time to recollect it all. He told himself he'd never meant to hurt anyone, but it didn't make him feel absolved.

His plan had been to hang around in the shadows near cash-points and wait until someone who looked like they were worth a fair bit of money came by. They won't miss a twenty or a ten, he told himself. He didn't like the idea of doing what he was doing, but if he really had to, he at least wanted some choice about it.

The trouble was that no rich-looking people had come by in the three hours he'd waited there.

Then somebody did come. It wasn't the stuck-up yuppie from the one per cent club that Glenn was hoping to find, but he was the only person he'd seen, so he pulled up his hood, took out the sushi knife he'd bought earlier that day, and crept up behind him. It was difficult to tell how big he was from the duffel coat, but Glenn grabbed him by the collar and dragged him down to the ground with little resistance. The man in the coat yelled for help and Glenn punched him in the stomach to knock the wind out of him. It worked.

"Money, now." Glenn had said. He made his voice sound gruffer than it really was. The guy tried to get up again, so Glenn made sure he could see the knife as he punched him in the stomach. To make sure he wouldn't resist, Glenn grabbed his hair and slammed the back of his head on the pavement enough times to leave a small spat of blood on it. When the guy was still Glenn started rummaging through his pockets. All he came out with was a crisp and uncreased twenty pound note.

What happened next, Glenn had not anticipated, nor did he fully understand how it happened.

His victim must have made a lunge to stand up while he was holding the note up to the light. Something pushed into his right hand, the hand that held the sushi knife, then it pulled him forward. Glenn looked down and saw his hand holding the knife, and the knife stuck in the man's throat. He choked and frantically tried to grab the handle of the blade. Glenn panicked, wrenched the knife out, dropped it, and watched the guy fall face first into the gutter next to the graffiti and rust-covered skip.

"There. Doesn't it feel good to tell the truth?" The Samuel in his head said, mocking him.

"I never meant to hurt anyone."

"You just keep telling yourself that. It'll make it all better."

"I just needed the money. To get them off my back for just one day."

There was no reply. The voice in his head was gone.

Glenn got up from the settee. Everything spun around him, slanted on its side, blurred out of focus, and he fell forwards. A churning pain grew in his stomach and when he coughed he could taste the vomit that was backing up down his throat. He crawled into the kitchen. When he made it to the sink the need to throw up had gone. His eyes stung with fresh tears, but he made out the two bottles of paracetamol near the sink with little trouble. The kitchen floor was cold and as he sat down, propped up against the fridge, he opened both the bottles and tipped the pills into his mouth, washing them down with the last of the whiskey.

He told himself he'd never meant to hurt anyone.

It was the sunlight pouring in from the unblinded kitchen window that woke him up. It must have been shining on him for a few hours, because his whole body was hot. He managed to open his eyes and loll his head to one side where the light didn't blind him.

He tried to move. He was weak. He must have been sick while he was passed out as there were a couple of pools of vomit at the side of him, some of it on him. Mixed in with the vomit was a lot of tablets.

When Glenn tried to sit up, that was when he felt the headache. A whole bottle of whiskey's worth of hangover hit him and he threw up again. This time it was mostly just bile. Unlike most hangovers where he remembered very little of the night before, this time Glenn remembered everything in graphic detail. Everything from the green edged letters from the council, to having a conversation with himself like he was talking to a ghost, right up to a minute or so after he swallowed all the tablets and everything went quiet. He lay still on the kitchen floor for a while, as he thought everything over.

The automatic doors hissed open as he neared, welcoming him inside. Everything from the ceiling to the floor was white. Some of it was patched with dust and scratches, but for the most part it was bright enough to make his eyes sting and remind him of the hangover he'd given himself. He didn't know if it was safe to take any more painkillers, so earlier he'd told himself he'd just have to grin and bear the headache.

Chairs were set in rows on the left hand side of the room and on the right, sitting behind a glass screen was a woman in a white shirt and black tie.

"Can I help you?" She said, looking at him.

You know, it's not too late to back out. You can still leg it. Nobody would know and nobody would blame you, said a voice in the back of Glenn's mind.

No.

Since when were you so altruistic?

I'm not being.

Please…

His heart raced as he sat down on the chair in front of the woman. He almost got up again, and had to force himself to stay seated. He said: "Good afternoon, constable. I've got something to tell you."

Sam Graham is 25 years old and from Hull in East Yorkshire, although he now lives in Preston, Lancashire. He has been writing for as long as he can remember. In 2011, he was commissioned by the EU to write a novel surrounding a hate-crime. While this novel is being edited, he is working on the second book. His favourite writers are Mickey Spillane and HP Lovecraft and aside from writing, he plays the guitar for a local rock band.

Photograph by Craig Lindop

THE FIRST FLOWER AFTER THE FLOOD

Issara 'Simonet' Edwards

I used to see God in the cracks, the little lapses of light that escape from shadows. I used to see a whole host of spectacular things. Now, of course, I'd be lucky to see what was going on two feet in front of me. Old age you see, it creeps up on you like slow-growing vines. It batters away at you, chipping away a bit more of your life and youth everyday... every second. You won't believe me of course, but you will. You'll see that time is heavy, crippling. I see it all the time; time takes its toll, as they say. Look out your window, see it in the way the old women hunch over their walking frame, like the world itself is upon their shoulders. So, like I said, time is heavy. Believe me, at eighty-four, time is very heavy on me.

As I sit on this warm spring day, waiting in my armchair that I remember being a vibrant green, now looking more brown, I confess, I almost feel like a child. Perhaps that's what it was about her, or maybe not. Maybe it was just her eyes. Yes. Definitely her eyes...

As the air gets colder, and my skin gets thinner, tired like the paper they use to roll cigarettes, I remember her eyes. There's a creaking sound as I get up from my chair to look out the window for her, and the travesty is I can't tell whether it's me creaking or that old chair of mine; probably a bit of both by now.

I feel like a bit of a curtain twitcher, like that old Mrs Burton over the road, as I peer out to catch a glimpse of her leaving the house, and skipping over to mine like she did so often in her youth.

The moment I saw her pull up it was like my heart caught in my throat. Her parents told me she was coming of course, but it was still something to see her. She drove up in one of those big modern cars; black with tinted windows… she always said she was going to make something of herself… my little angel from number 142. Her light hair bounced as she got out of the car, a white linen dress clinging to her. I expected her to turn, to see me in the window. I wanted to see that smile, that beam of delight that I would see every day before she moved away to college. The foolishness of an old man I suppose.

Her parents were overjoyed to see her, hugged her like it had been years… but it couldn't have been. I remember her like it was only yesterday… the light that haunted her green eyes, her small curved lips… just memories now. They're just darkness and whispers flying overhead, never touching, never landing… just distant lights in a distant sky. And yet, sometimes, my memories can feel more real to me than the beating of my heart.

I was a tailor. A very good one, I might add. I

made suits for businessmen, for weddings, Bar Mitzvahs, funerals, pageboys and once, just once, for a very special girl named Alice.

I was doing repairs that morning. Mr Akiro's wife had brought in a suit I'd made for him some time ago. Apparently the poor gentleman had been experiencing problems with the zipper. His poor blushing wife had come to me, trousers in hand, telling me that it would just roll down at the most inconvenient moments. The most recent time, she said, was when he was giving a speech at his cousins wedding. Really, the dear man needed a new suit, but was just too cheap to get one and it had been years since I'd stitched that one. Also, he wasn't at all as light as he was back then… how he was still squeezing into the thing, well… But I minded my tongue and said I would replace the zipper in no time at all.

I had just finished up and was placing Mr Akiro's trousers in one of the gold pattern boxes we put the new suits in for the customers to collect, when she bounced in with her parents. Nine years old and full of light and youth and beauty. The sun danced in her little blonde curls as she bounded towards me and it was as though all the air was sucked out of the room. Her eyes, they were full of fire, of light, of an intelligence that should not be bound by youth or held in the hands of a child.

I stood behind the counter, frozen; completely paralysed by the presence of her. She smiled at me, a broad, beautiful smile. Her mouth was covered in what appeared to be some kind of lip balm, a bright pink colour, making her look like sweets.

"Hello. I'm Alice, what's your name?"

I stood back, glancing up to see her parents, stood by the door, waiting, letting her take charge of this moment that she'd obviously been planning. Her little expectant face was looking up at me, still beaming, but I couldn't form any words. She was the most dazzling creature I had ever seen in my life, the glint in her eyes filling my entire being with an overwhelming sense of knowing. My mouth moved, but I still couldn't quite get anything out… but how could I disappoint her, those eyes begged a response.

"I… I… I… I'm, I'm Christopher... a, I mean, Mr Haught." I managed to stammer out, fixing my slicked back hair, suddenly worried about how I looked to this strange young girl. This magical girl that made me feel… something, yet I couldn't quite fathom it.

"Hello Mr Haught, I would like a suit please."

"Um… for your father?"

I heard chuckling from behind her.

"No, Mr Haught, for me." Her tiny hands reached up to hold the counter between us. "I'm doing a presentation at my school where we all have to dress up as what we want to be when we grow up, I want to be a lawyer… or um, what's the word mummy?" She said, turning to her mother who was fading further and further into the scenery.

"A barrister."

"Yeah, a ba-rr-ister. I saved up all my birthday money." She said excitedly as she emptied out the front pocket of her little yellow dress and poured the contents of it before me. Pennies mostly, with the odd fifty and twenty pound note crinkled up within it.

"My dad said he would pay for the rest if this isn't enough. He said it could be my other, other present."

"I'm sure I could. It could. I'm sure it could." I replied nervously.

I took her to the back to be measured; her parents still lingering behind, but staying back a respectable distance, still letting her remain in charge. Eventually, her parents drifted off as some phone call took precedent. It was just me and her.

My hands trembled as I took the measuring tape from one small shoulder to the next. Her eyes watched me intently, staring straight into mine as though I was the only person in the world, not wavering, not for a second. Only one other person in my life had looked at me in that way… and she was long gone.

She followed my hands as I adjusted the tape, my sweaty, shaky fingers loosing grip, almost dropping it. I managed to keep hold of one end, still fighting to stay in some sort of control, then I felt her hand wrap around mine. Kneeling before her, I looked up into her eyes, a smile spreading across her face.

"It's okay." She whispered. "You don't have to be scared of me." Her voice was like bells, so sure, so clear, whispering the same words, Marie's words. They were the words whispered to me on our first date, when we sat in the car on the way to the movies. My hands were shaking so much I could barely keep hold of the steering wheel… my Marie. The trembling subsided immediately, her will, hushing them away. Her presence filled with assurance, her voice, filling me with memory.

When her parents came back in, Alice was explaining to me that the suit had to be black, but that the inside could be a pretty colour, like blue, she hated pink, babies wore pink and she was anything but that. They left shortly after, her eyes lingering on me for longer than they should have. As the door to the shop closed behind her, the world became a dull shade of grey, at least, until later that evening.

I had gotten home late that evening, a few last-minute dash orders had come in, which at the time I had been grateful for, monotonous tasks to distract the mind so. Order after order had come in that day, and with only two tailors working, it was like they expected miracles. The young, they have no idea of the time and skill it takes to put an entire suit together, they think everything can be done at their whim and be delivered to them by *their* earliest convenience. Although, I was probably just the same in my younger days.

I parked the car in my driveway and was in the process of negotiating my key into the hole when I heard her voice. The sky was almost dark and for a moment, I thought that I must have been imagining it, what would a young girl be doing calling my name at this hour. But when I turned round, there she was, wearing a white flannel nightgown and running towards me like I was her knight in shining armour. Her mother was in the doorway across the road from me, waving, whilst at the same time unsuccessfully trying to summon her in.

"Mr Haught, Mr Haught, how's my suit? I've been waiting for you for hours; I wouldn't go to bed until I saw you."

'Of course.' I thought, suddenly realising why she seemed so familiar to me. Mr and Mrs Linbourogh's daughter. I remembered them coming home with her when she was born. How had I not noticed that she had grown so? I shoved my keys in the trouser pocket and bent down to talk to her.

"Hello Alice. It isn't quite finished yet…" I started, but for some reason, I couldn't quite lie to her. She was so like my Marie; I could never lie to her either.

"Well, truth be told, I haven't quite started yet, but I will, first thing tomorrow."

"Well, that's okay, I know you must be busy and I wouldn't want you to work too hard." She said, startling me into standing, back straight, reminding me of my days in school. Not even grown men were that considerate of my trade.

"Mr Haught?" She said, her voice bringing me back to her presence.

"Yes Alice."

"Would it be okay if I came over tomorrow, I had some more ideas about what colour I want the inside to be?"

"Of course. Oh, but don't you have school, I think my store closes just as you leave."

"Well, that's okay; I can come over to your house."

This girl was developing an uncanny habit of stunning me into silence.

"Oh, umm, you… well, you, you must ask your parents."

"Oh, there's no point, they work most days until about eight."

"Well, who looks after you?" I asked, my worried glare seeming to amuse her.

"I do. I can even make dinner." A remark with which I'm sure I was meant to be impressed with, but frankly I just found rather disturbing. Don't mothers stay home to take care of their children anymore?

"Well, if you want to, come over… that will be fine."

I consoled myself with the thought of at least giving her a proper meal, instead of whatever packet nonsense she was preparing for herself.

At five o'clock the next day, she was at my door. I'll admit, I did close up the store and send dear Frank home a little earlier than usual just so I could make our meeting, and she would later admit as well that she ran all the way from the bus stop just so I wouldn't think she broke her word.

We talked about the suit at first. Her skinny legs were hanging off the counter as she watched me dice the carrots for the stew. But soon the talk turned elsewhere.

"Jon Li. I want to marry Jon Li, when I grow up."

"Is he a pupil at your school?"

"No." She giggled. "He works with my Dad. He makes deliveries."

"Oh, he works with your father. Well, wouldn't he be a little old for you?"

"No, not when I grow up and I'm the same age as him."

"I don't think it quite works like that. If only it did."

"I don't think age matters when you get older, we'll both be old, right?"

"I suppose so." I muttered as I dropped the carrots into the simmering pot.

"So, why do you want to marry Jon Li?"

"I think he's wonderful. Every time I see him, I remember when he baked me cookies for my birthday."

"What flavour were the cookies?"

"Cherry and vanilla."

"That sounds about right." I said more to myself than her.

"Are you married Mr Haught?"

"No. I never did marry. There was someone once… but, we never quite managed to get down the aisle. No. I suppose I'm a bit too old for all of that now."

"Don't say that Mr Haught, you're very nice and you're obviously a very good cook; I'd marry you."

"Well, you're far too young to be talking like that - and what about your Mr Li? Weren't you engaged to him a few minutes ago?" I said to her in a flurry of words, my face turning red with embarrassment with every syllable.

"Oh, Mr Haught. I thought I told you, we'll both be old someday." She said as she jumped down of the counter and took the knife from me. She took the piece of rabbit that I had bought for this occasion and began chopping it with a skill I hadn't seen in years.

"I told you I could cook didn't I, Chrissy."

"What did you call me?" I asked, feeling every drop of blood draining from my body.

"I don't know." She replied nonchalant. "Shall I put the rabbit in now?"

I nodded, unsure of what else to do. Only Marie had ever called me that… her little round face teasing me because she knew how much I hated her pet name for me, her hazel eyes laughing… my fingers in her dark hair, teasing out the curls.

"She died didn't she?" Alice's voice snapped me out of the memory. "The girl you almost married."

"Yes." My voice drier, thicker than before.

"It's sad." She muttered to herself as she placed the lid on the pot. "What happened to her?"

"It was a car accident, on the way to the church. I waited… but she never came." I suddenly felt dizzy as I remembered that day; nausea filled my stomach, heat filling my face and head.

Alice rushed to me, guided me to a seat at the dining table and then took the seat opposite.

"I'm sorry, Mr Haught. I'm here now." She said, looking into my eyes and smiling.

When the suit was finished, she came over after school to show me how it looked. She had tried it on in the store with her parents, letting them snap pictures whilst she twirled. Yet then she had come over the day after, to show me how it looked with the correct shoes and her hair tied up neatly in a bun.

She came over again, the evening after the presentation, to tell me how it went and redo the entire presentation just for my benefit. And later, she would just come over. We would have dinner at five-thirty, watch TV until seven-thirty and I would walk her home by eight. It was a perfect time for both of us, like we existed for those moments only.

One night, we sat together on the sofa watching some American show that she found particularly amusing, she reached over and held my hand. It wasn't uncommon, in the months we'd known each other, she would often hold my hand as I walked her across the road, or brush lint from my attire if I had been especially careless with whatever fabric I had been working with that day. But the warmth in her hand felt different that day, like her very skin was flushed with the thought of what she was about to do next. I turned towards her, her eyes growing darker in the lamplight. She shuffled closer to me, tilting her head up and pressed her lips to mine. Softer than velvet and completely timeless.

I pulled away, taking her shoulders in my hands as gently as I could.

"What's the matter, did I do it wrong?"

"Yes. No. No, this is wrong."

"Don't you like me?"

"I do, like you very much… but you're too young. It's wrong, it just can't be"

"But it feels right… like I know you." She breathed, suddenly seeming so much older.

"I know." I muttered, not wanting to look at her, not wanting to give in.

"Then I'll wait. It feels like I've waited a long time anyway." She said, turning back to the TV.

It seemed that we lived like that for eternity, never touching, never straying into the obvious between us. We dwelled in this holding pattern, half alive, yet more alive with each other than we were without. I knew that there would be a day when she would outgrow me. Forget me, but even now, I hold that desire in my heart, the desire for her and her alone. It's like I had spent my whole life waiting for her, searching for her… like a ghost.

I heard the tapping at the door. Grabbing my cane, I walked to the door as fast as my old pins would let me. My hands trembled as I turned the latch and opened the door.

There she was, a vision in white, as always.

"Hello, Mr Haught."

"Alice." I breathed her name like a sigh of relief.

I reached out with my free hand to take hers, but instead she leapt forward and hugged me like I was the only man on Earth.

I sat down as she put the kettle on, still knowing her way around as though she never left. Less than five minutes later we sat on the sofa in front of the telly, hot cups of tea warming our hands as the open window blew in the chill spring air through the yellowing nets.

"So, I'm leaving tomorrow." She explained. She had just finished her medical degree in London and had gotten a position as an Aid Worker in Africa, at least until she got a proper job at a hospital. I couldn't have been more proud of her. Or more heartbroken.

"You must be so excited." I murmured into my tea, trying to be happy for her, and I was.

"I am. Disappointed though."

"Why's that?"

"I know this is a great opportunity but… it's gonna be so far away from you, and who knows, I might be needed out there for longer than a year."

"Oh, Alice." I said, putting my cup down as she placed hers on the coffee table. I took both her hands in mine and felt her breath as it brushed my face.

"Why is it that you're always too small, or too big?" She laughed, a breathless laugh, sorrow filling her eyes. She pressed her lips to mine, for the second and last time. The sweetest kiss I'd ever felt in my life. My Alice, all grown up, and off to explore the world.

I waved her off as she got in the car, driving off to her future. A future that this time would be filled with so much more than me… a future, leaving me with the past.

This is what I live for. The beautiful sentence. The universe that can exist in a single line of text. The infinity that can be seen in one perfectly crafted sentence. Issara 'Simonet' Edwards.

Photograph by Elle Hanley

AMONGST THE RUSHES

Hanne Larsson

I see a man with white, bushy hair, buttery brown eyes and a little puzzled smile looking back at me. He's wearing a grey suit- classic cut and could still be in vogue, except its buttons are straining and the trousers can't be done up. It is much too short in the leg.

"Maggie! The mirror doesn't lie; I can't wear this blasted costume! I may have looked dapper on our wedding day, but now I look an utter fool. Besides which, the tie always knew me for a fraud, and must be silently laughing at me." The old man frowns in the mirror and suddenly, I look like my pouting eight-year-old grandson when he's been told he can't have another piece of cake.

My wife's voice drifts up from the kitchen, "What do you mean it doesn't fit? We are not buying you a new suit for this occasion; it's money we don't have!"

I can hardly hear her through the floorboards but the gist is clear enough. It's her Standard Response 145: No Money for Nice Things.

For once I concur with her wisdom; I don't want a new suit. I hated wearing them for work and posh-dos. I begin by peeling off the jacket, slowly. My arthritic hands struggle to undo the buttons and one of them pings off, disappearing behind the furniture. And there it can stay; my back doesn't approve of being bent for more than 45 degrees any longer.

"Could I wear the clown suit instead?" I finally respond, the suit trousers puddling in a heap around my legs as I remember the box of dressing up clothes we keep in the loft. "It would be more fitting for the occasion, don't you think?"

"Have you finally lost your marbles, George? You can't go to Roy's funeral dressed as a clown!"

"But he *was* a clown, Maggie! A professional clown! He would have approved, I'm sure of it," I begin to wail, then stop, yet again reminded of my grandson's tantrums.

"Think of poor Iris, and their children; what will they think if you turn up in church with big shoes and a red nose? It's hardly the occasion," my wife's voice is getting closer, as if she's coming up the stairs to carry on the conversation without having to shout. I look down in panic at the mess on the floor and try to push it under the bed with my foot, but in so doing, my slipper comes off instead, adding to the pile.

"Well, what do you suggest? I can't wear this contraption, it looks worse on than that clown suit, and I see little point in buying a new one."

Maggie doesn't answer this one. Perhaps she is pondering how to get round the problem. She was always good at that, my Maggie. And they would always be cracking solutions. Like that time Pell, our long-haired tabby, got himself stuck in a pipe and no amount of pulling and coaxing managed to do anything but allow Pell to wedge himself further in. Maggie, with infinite patience, picked up the cooking oil, poured it all round the pipe from both ends, turning it over as she went, and then pushed a broom handle into the pipe. A rather greasy Pell fell into my lap. Arguably, the broom handle would have been enough, but I guess Maggie wanted some amusement for herself. She laughed herself into tears as I tried grabbing hold of the oiliest cat in our neighbourhood. This was closely matched by the good hour she then giggled at Pell trying to lick the oil off. She did take pity on him after that and used her best shampoo to get him clean. Mind you, Pell got his revenge and scratched her bloody in the bathroom.

"Any bright ideas?" I call out, rooting around for my cardigan and comfortable trousers that ended up somewhere in the bedroom when she first commanded me to try the hideous outfit on. Part of me concedes that she is right about the clown suit, but I remember so clearly the day Roy told me he was going to be a clown. We were eight years old, hanging on his front gate (something his father would later have an apoplectic fit about) and his voice was as serious as it had been when he had told me he would marry Iris from the next street over the summer before.

"Maggie? I *have* to wear the clown suit! Roy gave it to me when he retired; it was one of his spares," I begin again, hoping against all hope to convince her of this plan. Instead of her response, I hear an insistent knocking sound.

"Who's there? There's someone in the house, Maggie!" I try to hiss all this but only end up having a coughing fit. I look around for a weapon, reluctantly grabbing hold of the framed picture of my wife as a young woman in the Norfolk rushes examining a sailboat. It may stun the intruder for a moment.

"Mr. Danner? Are you alright? I could hear you talking to someone and then the coughing started," a young woman's voice calls out as she pokes her head round the door.

"Where's my suit?" I ask, looking for the puddle of grey I had left on the floor. "Where's Maggie? Why are you in my house?"

"Maggie isn't here any longer, Mr. Danner. Sit down, please," the woman with the firm voice raises a suspicion in me, gently taking the picture from my hand. "You remember, don't you? Today is Thursday, your daughter and grandson will be here soon to visit you."

As fast as I can, I whirl round, trying to find that suit, or the button, or my missing slipper. None of it is where I left it, and a wild hope rises in me- that I'll be able to wear that clown suit to Roy's funeral after all.

"I left my suit here, my wife asked, well, no, commanded that I try it on so that I could go to my best friend's funeral. But it didn't fit, and there's no money to buy a new suit," I sit down heavily on the bed, "but if Maggie isn't here to tell me what to wear, then I can go get the clown suit from the loft! Excuse me, miss, I won't be a minute."

My hand is on the doorknob when the final scene snaps into focus. And then, yes, then, I do remember. I remember where I am. It is as if the film has run out in my head and all I'm left with is the blackness at the end of the reel. That searing white light that shines in my eyes when the reel is removed from its spool is my reality. The young woman sits down next to me, holding my hand. I want to thank her and curse her but all the words have abandoned me. Gently, I take the photograph back from the woman. I didn't take many things when I went into the care home, but the picture of my wife holding a sailboat has always come with me. She was the young one, the bright one, and now I'm here by myself.

"There, there, Mr. Danner, everything will be alright," the woman soothes, stroking my hand. "You've got visitors to look forward to."

"It won't be the same," I reply, hugging the frame to my chest, tears flowing down my wrinkles. "Maggie was the one that cheered my world."

Hanne Larsson is a 29-year-old Swede, living in Reading, who doesn't write crime novels. She has finally begun to get some motivation and focus on her writing after years of dabbling on the backs of envelopes, and has at least 4 notebooks on the go at any one time. She writes fantasy novels, short stories and attempts poetry. When she doesn't, she enjoys observing her neighbourhood's colourful characters, baking and playing addictive board games with friends.

Photograph by Michel Nguie

MARCY

ELLIE STEWART

There had been no rainfall for seven months, and it was the hottest summer anyone could remember. The waters had all retreated, the rivers shrivelled, the stream that ran alongside the fields had shrunk to a damp trickle that dribbled by the grass husks as if it were gasping for breath.

We lived in a house on the edge of the village that backed onto a field. As I child, I had spent summer days racing round it with friends and riding my bike over the uneven ground. My parents held barbecues that went on into the evening, and we would camp right beside the house and wake up when the sun rose. Now I was old enough to drink at these occasions, and my friends and I would sit around the fire far from the laughter and chattering of my parents and their guests, swigging cider and playing guitar into the long, long hours.

But this summer had been too hot; the field was parched. The dry grass crackled and snapped when you stepped on it, burnt bare feet and reflected the white sun. There had been no rain, there had been no clouds. Our sprinkler spluttered over the lawn in our garden in the day, and in the evenings we ate dinner at the outside table and listened to the crickets sing.

One day, just after noon, I came running back from the field, flung open the back door, and picked up the phone.

I called Marcy.

"Hello," she said.

"Marcy, you have to come round," I said. "There's something you've gotta see."

Marcy arrived half an hour later, and dropped her bike on our front lawn. Her hair was white-blond and her nose freckled. She hardly ever wore make-up.

"I'm here Danny," she called as she stepped into the hall.

"Hey!" I said, running down the stairs.

"Hello Marcy," said my mother, drying her hands on a tea towel as she stepped from the kitchen.

"Hello Pam," she said.

"I've got some things for you to take back with you when you head home," she said.

"Thank you," said Marcy, and smiled.

I pulled on my shoes.

"Come on," I said.

The field rose upwards and then sloped down out of sight from the house. It was a good place to hide from my parents when friends came over to smoke a joint or when I, professing my desire to be alone for a few hours, would take my ruck-sack and head over the hill, to swig whiskey and smoke, write poetry or read magazines and rub myself to a muffled groan out in the empty field that changed colours as the light faded.

We walked through the field, away from the house.

"This summer has been so long," said Marcy, shielding her eyes from the sun.

"Yeah," I said.

I loved Marcy, of course. I had known her since we were five, and we had gone through the stages of playing as children, of hostility as we became more aware of gender and then the difficult first years of high school when we were both terrified, and lonely, and found one another again. One day I found myself noticing the brightness of her eyes and the length of her legs, and after that I began to notice the way her body moved under the fabric of her clothes. I longed to hold her and kiss her, more than anything. I assumed she wasn't aware.

We reached the curve of the hill and looked down across the dry grass.

In the middle of the field was a refrigerator.

It was white, just over five-foot high, glittering in the sun and unmoving.

We walked down the slope and stood in front of it. It looked utterly ordinary, if a little battered round the edges. Apart from our home, there wasn't a house around for miles.

"What is it doing here?" said Marcy.

"I don't know," I said.

We stood still and listened to the insects chirping in the dead grass.

"How did it get here?"

I shrugged.

She looked up.

"Do you think it fell from the sky?"

I looked at her. Her hair fell down in fronds onto her shoulders, which were dappled by the sun.

"I don't know," I said. "It's strange."

Marcy pulled open its door. There was nothing inside. She shut it again.

"Someone must have dragged it here and left it," she said.

"Why would they do that?" I said.

We looked up. The sky was bright blue. There were no clouds.

"Maybe it did fall from the sky," she said.

"Maybe." I said.

She looked at me, and smiled.

When we got back to the house, my mother had a bag waiting for Marcy.

"Honey, there are two meals in here for you: lasagne and beef stew. They'll last for a couple of days in the fridge, so it's probably a good idea to put one in the freezer."

"Thank you, Pam," said Marcy, picking up the bag.

"Mum-" I said.

"Oh, you cycled here, didn't you?" she said, suddenly realising. "Well, I'll drive you home."

"No, you don't have to-"

"Of course! Now where are my keys…"

Mum pulled off her apron and went to find the keys.

I smiled at Marcy.

"Come back tomorrow," I said. "If you like. To see if it's still here."

Marcy laughed.

"OK," she said.

I looked at my feet.

"Is she in the hospital Saturday?" I said.

"Yeah," she said.

"I'll come by then," I said.

"OK."

Mum came out of the kitchen, jangling the car keys before her.

"Got them!" she said, beaming.

Marcy's mum was dying. She had been diagnosed with cancer a year earlier, but chemotherapy hadn't worked. It had come back: they found it in her lungs. Marcy had a younger brother, and her father barely knew how to cook. Mum made them meals as often as she could. I never knew what to say to Marcy, but I was there for her after every hospital visit.

I don't know what Marcy saw when she looked up into the blank blue sky.

I spent the evening sitting on the hill, watching the refrigerator as the sun sank slowly away. That summer, we spent days and evenings in that field. Our friends all gathered, and we set up tents around the refrigerator. We burnt a fire in front of it, and sang drunken songs.

After a few weeks, the nights grew colder. A wind began to blow.

One morning, I crawled from my tent in the bare morning air and saw Marcy sitting cross-legged in front of the refrigerator. Hungover, still slightly drunk, I crawled over to her. I smiled, but then she turned to me with tears in her eyes.

"I don't want mum to die," she said, and started to cry.

I pulled her to me and held her tightly. She dug her fingers into me and sobbed. It was an animal sound of terrible pain. All her muscles tensed. I kissed the top of her head.

"What does it mean?" she said, "Why does she have to die?"

I shook my head. I clenched my teeth. I didn't believe in God, so there was no one to be angry at. I held her tighter. She pressed herself into me hard, and I felt her bones.

"I don't know," I said.

She pulled away from me and scrubbed hard at her eyes. Something fell from her pocket, and reflected the light of the rising sun. I leant over and picked it up. It was a cross on a gold chain.

"Is this yours, Marcy?" I said, holding it in my palm.

"Yes," she said, suddenly still.

She took it from my hand and lowered her head. She sniffed.

"I didn't know you were religious," I said, softly.

I lowered my head, trying to see her face. I wanted her to look at me.

"I don't think I am," she said.

"So what does that mean?" I said, pointing to the cross that she held in her hands, the fine chain running over her fingers.

"I don't know," she said, and looked up.

Her eyes were wide, and bright blue. They shimmered with her tears, but her face was so still.

"I don't know," she said again.

Then she smiled.

"Hope," she said.

Ellie Stewart grew up in Wimbledon and Tunbridge Wells, and studied English and Philosophy at The University of Leeds. She has been published in various places online, blogs for The Huffington Post and her stories have been published by Ether Books as an app. Ellie currently lives in South East London.

Photograph by Natia Rekhviashvili

THE END

Eve Murray

Her eyes were dry and burned in her head. Beatrice watched as her room limped from the deep charcoal of night into the bleached chalk of a summer's morning. Another sleepless night. She reached over and turned off her alarm before it broke the morning's silence. She rose from the covers and stepped between the grease-lined take-away boxes that swelled around her bed and lit a cigarette.

The kitchen floor stuck to her naked feet as she filled the kettle and poured coffee into her stained cup. The milk was off, so she drank it black. It spilled as she placed it on her desk in the study, a new ring seeped into the wood.

Every waking moment of the last three and a half years had been spent with him. Now there was nothing. Just the relentless increase in time separating her from him. It had already been five days since she killed him. Five tormented days and four despairing nights. His absence rotted through her, a cancer gorging to the core leaving an aching hollow.

She knew from the beginning how it would end. Still she chose to let him back into her life, to open that painful chapter. Every day in his company edged him closer to his demise.

The most painful bit was over. Now she needed to focus on why. She had two weeks to answer that question, to draw her conclusions and end this 'story' - preferably in ten pages or less. Her publisher and editor had already given her an extension and their patience was thinning daily.

They often joked with her about how her main characters never made it to the final chapter. They would ask for the body count with a smile before asking for a synopsis. They didn't know that this was different. She hadn't told them that the central character of Magnus was based on her brother.

Magnus was 17 when he killed himself, she was eleven. They were living with their gran in a little cottage along the coast, near the fishing village of Nochnar. She awoke to the sound of her grandmother's screams echoing through her bedroom window. She threw open the curtains and looked outside. Dawn was raw on the horizon and hung in torn shades of red. The land lay in silhouettes sheltered from daybreak by the rise to the clifftop. Something white moved in the fading darkness. She only caught a glimpse before it disappeared from view, masked by her window frame. It reappeared in the next pane a couple of seconds later. It was her gran in her nightdress, frantically wading through the long grass at the foot of the rise. Instinctively Beatrice thought her gran was hurt, she was about to rush out to help her when she realized she was headed away from the house. She looked in the direction that her gran was moving towards, searching for the answer. She found it. In her top left window pane, framed like a photograph of a treasured memory, stood the black outlines of the old tree etched on dawn's wounded light. Below it hung the shadow of her brother.

That was thirteen years ago but she was reliving it as if it were yesterday. The pain was sharp again, no longer rounded to a dull ache by the passage of time. She had wanted to write him down from the branch but she wasn't the creator of this story, just a witness. Still, if she hadn't written that last line, he would still be with her, in some sense. She felt him fading as she wrote it. Growing paler with each typed word. By the time she reached the full stop, he was gone. He died all over again only this time she felt responsible.

The phone rang in the hallway. She made no attempt to answer it. She knew it would be Pam, her publisher, checking in and checking up on yesterday's progress. There hadn't been any. She left her to the answering machine.

The book was written from several perspectives, her own, her gran's, friends of her brother and her brother's. The hope was to fill in the blanks and get a more rounded view of who he really was. Maybe then she would find the answers. She needed something to cushion the pain. A frail consolation of some kind of understanding.

They were trapped beneath his long cast shadow. All he had left them was guilt, anger and a devastation that corroded through their lives. His absence was always present between them. It's funny how that happens, how the lack of someone can be more noticeable than the presence of those still there.

She fell victim to his suicide and became lost inside her grief. She was known as "that girl whose brother killed himself" rather than Beatrice. Whoever she was supposed to be, whatever potential she had, died when he stepped off that branch.

Her gran never looked at her the same after his death. Beatrice looked so like him that it became hard to see her. Sometimes when her gran thought she was asleep, she would sit on the edge of the bed and gently sweep the hair from her face. "There you are" she'd whisper, her words soaked in whiskey "I miss you". Beatrice never said anything. She just lay there beneath the mask of Magnus and felt herself dissolve.

She felt this pressure, this unspoken desire for her to be like him. She knew it gave her gran comfort to see glimpses of him in her. It eased her suffering. So she picked up his life as best she could and lost her own in the process.

That's why she became a writer; it's what Magnus wanted to be. He was never without a notebook in his pocket and a pencil behind his ear. He could find poetry in the most mundane things and reveal it in a way that humbled his readers for not noticing. He wrote with such clarity and grace. That's what made it all the more painful that he never left a suicide note.

In the days that followed his death, their gran had searched his room. Beatrice remembered hearing her shuffling around, moving things about through her bedroom wall. She crept down the hall and peered through the doorway. Her gran sat on the floor surrounded by his notebooks she had emptied from a box she found under his bed. The floorboard creaked beneath Beatrice's foot as she stepped inside. "It's late" her gran said without looking at her "go back to bed". Beatrice turned and walked back to her room. The darkness swelled behind her, each step smudged her into nightly shades.

The next morning, whilst her gran was still sleeping, she snuck into Magnus's room. There on the bed stacked and waiting were five of his notebooks along with the unspoken understanding that this is all she would be getting. She was grateful to have them but she knew all these stories. She wanted to know what was in the others and why they were being kept from her.

They never spoke about the notebooks, even though they both knew that Beatrice was looking for them and her gran was reading them. Why else would her gran have suddenly started locking her bedroom door? Night-time was the worst. "Sweet dreams," she would say as she turned off the bedroom light. Beatrice would listen to her footsteps as they walked down the hall to her own bedroom. There would be the slightest of pauses. The soft thud of the door as it closed. Then the sharp sting of the key as it turned in the lock. She hated that sound. It was the sound of a grudge forming.

When she was twenty, her gran had to be moved into a care home. Beatrice had tried to look after her but her dementia had worsened and she could no longer cope. She moved from room to room hollowing the house of her grans possessions. Packing them into cardboard boxes that crowded the hallway. The only room left was the bedroom. Beatrice turned the handle; the door was stiff and reluctant to open, as though it knew it were her. She pushed it hard and it scrapped open over the carpet. "How long had this been unlocked?" she thought to herself. She had given up so long ago it could have been years. She stepped inside as though she were walking on a frozen river. Every step slow and precise, careful of sudden movements that could fracture its fragility. Her gran shuffled in behind her and sat on the bed, her finger traced the printed flower on the bed sheet. "Not long now gran, nearly done". She busied herself emptying her bedside cabinet not wanting to appear eager to find them. A fluttering grew in her stomach. She knew there were only three places they could be, under the bed, in the old trunk, or in the wardrobe. She approached each in a casual kind of a way pretending she was interested in nothing but the task at hand. All the time her eyes scanning.

Anticipation sweated through her as she lifted the lid on the trunk. She kept expecting her gran to say something but she never did. She held her breath as the light from the room poured in revealing that old cardboard box stacked with his notebooks. She just stood there for a moment staring at them, scared that any movement towards them may somehow alter their existence. Slowly, she reached in and picked up the box. Its structure softened and sagged in her grip. She lent it against her body and embraced it with all the delicacy that one might hold a newborn.

Still her gran said nothing. Perhaps she hadn't noticed, Beatrice thought to herself. It was stupid that she wanted her to. As it stood she could have just walked out the room with them. It's what she would have done years ago but it didn't feel right now. Part of her wanted permission. "Gran." Her gran lifted her head as frail as an autumn leaf and gazed at Beatrice with eyes as empty as a reflection. This was where her gran would speak; she would acknowledge the box and they would talk about it for the first time. But that pregnant pause never birthed such a conversation. Instead a silence grew that withered all hope. The room softened to a blur as Beatrice realized the depths of her gran's illness.

The cottage was sold to pay for her gran's care. Beatrice moved into a caravan in a nearby campsite. She visited her gran every day, and every night she sat at her foldaway table and read her brother's notebooks. The pages were soft and worn, some were crimped in patches where tears had dried. Three of the notebooks contained stories and poems that her gran would have deemed too adult for her. The other three were his journals that she never knew he wrote. She found him amongst the pages. The real him. Not the sugar coated image of the big brother she knew.

He wrote in heated shades of frustration about how he felt suffocated in this small town. How every day that passed stole a little more of him leaving him paper-thin. His words were stained with his impatience to escape, but his sentences formed the nagging reality that he had no means of doing so.

His images were dark and bereft of the beauty for which he was renowned. These journals stood in stark contrast to his other writings. Beatrice wept, believing that she had finally found the answer to the question that had stalked her for years. She opened her notebook and started writing. This would be a place where he could exist in all his shades and not just in the rose tint of his baby sister. A resting place for his soul.

That was three and a half years ago. Life had changed. She had lost her gran, moved to the city and published four books. But she still hadn't finished penning his grave. She had let Pam read it six months ago just to get some general feedback. She had gotten really excited, started talking about deadlines and launches. Beatrice hadn't wanted to write this book to a particular deadline but maybe she needed to. Most of the book was written and she had her layout for the final chapters. She agreed to have it finished for the end of August.

It was when she reached the last chapter that her story started to unravel. This was to be written from her brother's perspective, using his own words taken from his journals. It would be the suicide note that he never left explaining why he did it. She thought she had discovered why, but as she started to write, the reason seemed disconnected from the truth. She remembered some of the interviews she had had with his friends. They had confirmed his frustrations, but they had also spoken of their own at that time. When she thought about it, she too had felt that way. Some of her own journal entries from that age sounded very similar. Wasn't that just part of being a teenager, in particular a teenager from a small village? She knew that spike of discontent. The heat of frustration that spreads like infection. She recognized the ache that swelled through him like a hunger demanding more. More independence, more experiences, just more from life in general. She had been so desperate that she had embraced this as the answer and ignored how normal it in fact was.

So there she was with no end to her book and no end to her torment. She lit another cigarette and watched as a gray cloud formed above her. His notebooks lay scattered across her desk. They were of no use to her now. They covered his life; what she needed was his death. She looked at her watch. It was 9 o'clock, if she left now she could be in Nochnar before 7 pm. She threw on yesterday's clothes, grabbed her manuscript, and jumped in the car.

The air was hot inside, baked by the summer's sun. It hung from her body in dampened patches. The sun grew stronger as the miles rattled away. By midday the world was a mirror and Beatrice's head throbbed from it's reflected light.

She pulled into a small cafe on the edge of the motorway to rest her eyes from their sculpted squint and down some painkillers. She sat at the counter as the waitress served her her half-star meal of burger and chips that tasted of nothing but heat, and thumbed through her manuscript looking for inspiration. Her oily fingers smearing the page transparent beneath her touch.

A middle aged man, no doubt a trucker, sat at the far end of the counter. His body hung in bulges of fat like a melted candle left to harden. It was clear from his demeanor that he was a regular. He ate and spoke loudly, his mouth a washing machine of chewed food and spit that speckled the counter as he passed judgment on all that entered. The staff tolerated him politely through gritted smiles.

Beatrice rested her head in her hands in a way that covered her ears and tried to concentrate. "Look at the state of it", he said to no one in particular, "imagine having to go home to that. It's like something out of a horror film." Beatrice glanced in the mirror behind the counter and saw that his ketchup-licked finger was pointing to her. She turned to face him. The itch of her irritation rose to match the temperature of the room. "Excuse me?" "All I'm saying sweetheart is stick on some slap and maybe try smiling once in a while that's all." Wrong day, she thought to herself as she put the manuscript back into her bag. A red lipstick rolled out. She had forgotten that was in there. It was a prop she had bought to help her get in the mindset of Nancy, the main character from her last book. She traced the contours of her mouth as sensually as she could as she walked towards him with all the forced sexuality she could muster. She slowly ran her finger along the soft wet of her mouth "Is that better?" her voice soft and breathy. He couldn't say anything, but there was a glint in his eye and she knew she had him. "Do you know what I'm going to do to you?" His mouth and eyes widened as she closed her lips around her finger and pushed it deep into her mouth. He didn't notice the retching noise, just the hot splatter of sick as it landed in his lap. "You have a nice day now sweetheart," she said with a wink as she wiggled her way to the door. When she reached it, she turned back and blew a kiss into the stunned silence of the room.

The rest of the journey was uneventful. She reached Nochnor a little after seven and pulled up in the shadow of the hill ten minutes later. She stepped from her car into the long grass that her gran had waded through. The tree loomed down at her. If she closed her eyes she could still see him there. His gentle sway and spin as the breeze took him.

She felt the rough bark beneath her hand, the dips and falls of carved messages left by his friends. "We miss you" "We love you" "R.I.P" the usual generic sentiment. A hole had been drilled into the trunk at some point, she wasn't sure by who. They used to put a candle in it on his birthday and at Christmas. It seemed normal at the time. She looked up at the circular face of the stump where the branch used to be. Two men from the village had come and sawn it down three days after he hung himself, as if it were the mere convenience of the branch that had made him do it.

She doesn't remember but she used to play here as a child, swinging and spinning on the rope swing. Feet high in the horizon. Picking daisies as she swooped towards the ground. Those memories were blocked now. The only flowers she remembers picking were the ones she lay on his grave.

She sat and looked at the tree as the light softened around her. Its scars all chiseled by Magnus's death sat painful in her own body. She slowly started to realize that there was nothing that could heal those wounds. The search for answers just like her search for his notebooks were no more than a distraction. The possession of either could never lessen her loss.

She pulled her manuscript from her bag and opened it at the last page. It wasn't the ending she had expected. It fell away suddenly like the edge of the cliff. All the momentum lost in one step. It's that abruptness that made it perfect. "The End" she wrote. She burned a hole into the paper with her cigarette. The final full stop.

The End

Eve Murray has written poetry from when she was a child but has only recently branched into writing short stories, after taking an evening class in creative writing. She has since created Scribbling Arts, an Edinburgh based writing group that meets once a week to share stories.

Lightning Source UK Ltd.
Milton Keynes UK
UKOW041229240912

199540UK00001B/8/P

9 789963 706501